the NEW
su
cree

BOOK
5

The Case of the
Loony Cruise

Pauline Hutchens Wilson
Sandy Dengler

MOODY PRESS
CHICAGO

Library of Congress Cataloging-in-Publication Data

Wilson, Pauline Hutchens.
   The case of the loony cruise / Pauline Hutchens
Wilson and Sandy Dengler.
      p.cm. –(New Sugar Creek Gang ; 5)
   Summary: When eleven-year-old Les and his family,
accompanied by his friends in the New Sugar Creek
Gang and an uncooperative young family guest, take
a trip on a houseboat through Voyageurs National Park,
Minnesota, their faith helps them meet the challenges
they encounter.
   ISBN 0-8024-8665-7
   [1. Vacations–Fiction. 2. Houseboats–Fiction.
3. Emotional problems–Fiction. 4. Christian life–
Fiction. 5. Voyageurs National Park (Minn.)–Fiction.
6. Minnesota–Fiction.] I. Dengler, Sandy. II. Title.

PZ7.W69758 Caq 2001
[Fic]–dc21

                                        00-069246

                  1 3 5 7 9 10 8 6 4 2

         Printed in the United States of America

INTRODUCTION

I t just isn't the same."

My dad sounded so sad. We stood on the walkway of a freeway overpass, looking out across a sea of new houses. Miles of houses, street after street.

"That line of trees out there is Sugar Creek." He waved an arm toward the hives of condos. "All this used to be farmland. When Paul Hutchens wrote those books about the Sugar Creek Gang, this is the area he wrote about. Right here."

I'm eleven, and, according to Dad, I'm older than most of the *homes* out here. "At least there's still a Sugar Creek," I said. "How far is it from our new place?"

"Couple miles. But the past—that was another world." He looked at me. "I'm sorry the fun is gone."

Dad walked down the slope to our car. I fell in behind him, wishing he didn't feel so sad.

When I was little, he read to me every night. And my favorite books to read were about a bunch of kids called the Sugar Creek Gang. They lived on farms near a creek and had a zillion adventures, mostly out in nature somewhere.

When Dad switched jobs, he found out we were going to move into the very area where the stories took place. He got all excited. I think he expected to find those farms here yet.

He grew up on a farm, so he knows a lot about that stuff. Every few pages, Dad would stop reading and say, "Now, Les, let me tell you about—," and then he'd explain something about spiders or shitepokes or whatever the story was talking about. So good old Les—that's me—learned a lot about farm life and nature when I was little, even though we lived in town.

We drove back to our brand-new home. It was an older house on a shady little back street. Just then it was full of boxes that the moving van had dumped the day before. And I mean full. Not very homey yet, but our beds were put together and made up, so who needs more?

Early next morning, I put on my jacket and found my helmet. It took me a while to dig my bike out of the garageful of jumbled stuff. Then I rode off, headed west.

So Dad thought the fun was gone. I wasn't so sure. That broad strip of trees along the creek looked awfully inviting.

I figured maybe I could find something interesting there. So that's how it all started.

I never guessed that I'd get all wrapped up in a real, true adventure like the ones we'd read about. And I would never *ever* have guessed that the Sugar Creek Gang would come back.

PAULINE HUTCHENS WILSON

1

People who make movies have no imagination. I learned this from Noah, who ought to know what he's talking about.

My friend Noah goes to movies a lot. He says it's job training and he's going to be a movie reviewer when he grows up. Don't you believe it. He just likes to goof off.

Anyway, he says that when you hear some exotic bird call in a jungle movie, it's almost always either a loon or a kookaburra. Kookaburras live in people's backyards in Australia, and loons are our feathered friends of the far north. Nowhere near a jungle. In other words, the movie bird calls are not only fake but ridiculous. You would think that moviemakers would use—you know—a local tropical bird, whatever it is. Nope. Loons and kookaburras.

This didn't mean much to me, since I don't get around to going to movies. But then, for the first time, I heard a loon call drifting across a Minnesota lake to me. I understood. They're exotic, all right, and eerie. And amazing. Exactly what you'd expect in a dark, mysterious jungle.

The whole Sugar Creek Gang was visiting in Minnesota with my family and me, and we all listened to the loon. They liked the sound as much as I did. The only person who did not seem to like it was Lisa Glenn. But then, you can't imagine what a piece of work that girl was!

Just wait till I tell you about her.

I can't believe that we Sugar Creekers once envied her.

It all started one evening as our family was sitting at dinner. I was bored. You see, at my house, you can only talk about certain things while you're at the table. Pleasant things. Gross stuff is out. So is gossip (but then, we're not allowed to gossip anytime). Now I ask you: If you can't discuss snakes, road kill you happened across that day, and rumors about the neighbors, what's left to talk about? That leaves school, and this was summer vacation. In other words, I had nothing to say.

But that doesn't mean we ate in silence. Oh my, no! My two sisters—Hannah, almost fifteen, and Catherine, twelve—can fill any silence known to man.

Finally, Mom interrupted their nonstop chatter to announce, "You remember my friend Myrna, the one who owns a tourist camp up in Minnesota? She called today. A client canceled, she said, and a houseboat is available. She wants to know if we'd like to come up for a week in the park."

"What park?" Hannah asked between mouthfuls.

"Voyageurs National Park on the Canadian

border. It's named for the men who paddled freight canoes through that area almost two hundred years ago."

"And now houseboats go there, huh?"

"It's quite a deal. You rent a houseboat and cruise out through the park. There are campsites on shore just for houseboats."

Catherine asked, "Will there be other kids?"

Hannah asked, "Will there be electricity?"

And I asked, "When can we go?"

Dad—Bill Walker to outsiders—frowned. "The only problem I can see may not be a problem. I had a long talk with Joe in the office today. He's going to Europe for a work project, and his wife is on a medical mission in Central America."

"That sounds exciting," Mom said.

"Central America! Wouldn't that be a great place to visit!" I love to travel—not that we do it much.

"She's not just visiting. She's working in a hospital there. Anyway, Joe asked if his daughter could stay with us while they're both out of the country. She's about your age." Dad looked at Hannah.

What could Hannah say? No, no, Daddy, don't do it?

She glared squarely at me. "Sure! I'd love to have someone intelligent to talk to once."

"Whaddaya mean?" I protested. "I'm a real intelligent talker. I just don't talk about the same stuff you do. And you don't like to hear about snakes and fighter planes."

We were allowed to discuss fighter planes at the table. Not snakes. They're on the "gross" list.

And, I might add right here, I was not the one who made the list.

Dad continued, "The problem is that Lisa might be with us during the dates we'd be in Minnesota."

Mom shrugged. "We can easily take her along. In fact, I was thinking we might invite your friends, Les. Your Sugar Creek Gang."

"Wouldn't Tiny love to go! He's never been to Minnesota, and he'd add lots of new birds to his bird list. And Mike and Lynn and Bits! That would be sterling!"

Hannah wrinkled her nose. "Sterling?"

I just sort of smiled. "The latest word, Hannah. Don't you keep up?"

OK. I confess. I doubt anyone Hannah's age in that town ever heard that word, except when it described silver. But Hannah was always so proud of being up on the latest of everything, I just loved to throw her a curve every now and then.

So that's how Lisa Glenn came to stay with us for a couple weeks. And that's how we all went to Minnesota.

I thought that it would be pretty uneventful out on a houseboat, with nothing much to do but mess around and maybe fish a little.

Boy, was I ever wrong.

2

Just as I tooled into the Sugar Creek County Park picnic area on my bike, a squirrel came racing across the grass in front of me. And right behind it flew a mockingbird. I mean right behind. The squawking bird was fluttering along very low to the ground, pecking at the squirrel. And the panicky squirrel was trying its level best to run faster than the speed of sound or whatever it would take to get away from the bird.

At the picnic table where we Sugar Creekers met, the rest of the gang sat laughing at the two critters. Tiny perched on the table with his feet on the bench, watching the squirrel through binoculars. He knew everything there was to know about animals and plants and natural history. His real name is Clarence Wilson, but he tries to keep it a secret.

Lynn was laughing so hard she had tears. Lynn Wing is Chinese and Japanese and the smartest person you'll ever meet. But no one knows that she's so smart because she's so quiet. And now that I think about it, that's pretty smart.

Elizabeth "Bits" Ware was laughing, too, but she doesn't get amused much by animals.

She likes electronics. When your computer's on the fritz, she's the one to call.

Mike Alvarado is not the one to call. He's all thumbs with computers. A computer sees him, and it instantly locks up. But he can tear a lawnmower motor apart and put it back together correctly when it's too dark in the evening to see. I've watched him do it.

That was us, the Gang. We all looked pretty usual, except for one of us. It wasn't Tiny, who's black. He was the tallest and the thinnest, but otherwise normal. Lynn was . . . well . . . basically Asian looking, I guess, with straight black hair and dark, gentle eyes. Bits was totally ordinary, with plain brown hair and eyes. Mike Alvarado had Mexican parents.

I'm the one who's not usual. I have bright red hair and freckles, and there aren't many of us true carrot tops.

Mike pointed toward the tree the squirrel had just climbed. "You should've seen it, Les! The squirrel must have climbed too close to the bird's nest. All of a sudden it comes boiling down outta that tree over there and across the lawn and up this other tree. Right past all of us. And the bird on its tail the whole way!"

Tiny asked, "What's this about Minnesota? I didn't quite get what you said in your e-mail."

"A week on a houseboat, and Mom and Dad want to take you guys too. My dad's calling your folks right now to ask permission. And there's going to be another girl with us, a Lisa Glenn."

Bits gaped. "*Lisa Glenn!* Why in the world do they want to take *her?*"

"You know her?"

"Everybody at school knows her. She's always in hot water. She's been caught smoking, and cheating, and stealing. And she's a world-class snob. She thinks she's so much better than everyone, just because she has tons of fancy clothes and pierced ears and all that. Her nose is stuck up in the air so far that she's gonna inhale a 747 one of these days. Les, if she comes along, we won't have any fun at all."

Now, this was something I hadn't heard before.

Tiny nodded. "How'd that happen?"

"Her dad works in the same law office as my dad. The way Dad was talking, she's a straight A student. Real popular."

"Straight A!" Bits sniffed. "She's a straight T. T for Trouble!"

I wondered for a moment why Dad would think Lisa was so great. Then I realized his lawyer friend, Lisa's father, probably thought she was the greatest thing since jack cheese. Mr. Glenn would brag about his daughter, and Dad would assume it was true—or that most of it was true. I tended to believe Bits more than Lisa's father.

Anyway, we started making plans. We chained up our bikes and walked back around the Swamp Trail to a little place on the creek bank. There the dragonflies zipped around. The ants scurried all over, carrying stuff. The birds sang. Turtles basked on a log out in the creek. And we sprawled out on the shore to make lists.

Tiny babbled on and on about the wonderful birds in the far north. Most of all, he said, he wanted to see a loon.

Mike wanted to know what kind of motor the houseboat had. Lynn and Bits started putting together a grocery list. The first three items were graham crackers, marshmallows, and chocolate bars for making s'mores.

We made a list of addresses to send postcards to—their folks, some aunts and cousins —so that we wouldn't leave anyone out.

Being with the Sugar Creek Gang on a summer afternoon in the park was about the best time a boy could have. Tiny wasn't the only naturalist; he was just the most enthusiastic. We all enjoyed being out in nature.

A kingfisher came through. It would park on a branch out over the water just downstream and watch awhile. Suddenly it would plunge straight down off the branch into the water, as if it had just accidentally fallen off. Almost instantly it would fly back up to its perch. A silver minnow would be flapping in its beak. Sometimes, down the hatch the fish would go. Other times, the bird would fly off with its fish, probably to feed little birds.

And I remembered what Noah said about loon and kookaburra calls in movie places where they would never be. Our kingfisher here at Sugar Creek and those kookaburras out in Australia were close relatives. The only real difference was, this one didn't make that crazy, maniacal laugh that kookaburras do.

Around suppertime we broke up the meeting, and I headed home. As I rolled into our front yard and dumped my bike, a big sports utility vehicle pulled up to the curb.

The driver, a short, stocky, pleasant-looking man, climbed out and hurried around to the back. He opened the hatch and said, "Come on, Gerty!"

Gerty hopped to the ground.

I fell in love with Gerty instantly. She was a big black Labrador retriever, kind of clumsy, all wags and happy licking. Gray hairs around her muzzle told the world that she was getting up in years, but you'd never guess it from the way she bounced around so eagerly.

Mom and Dad came out of the house and down the walk, but the driver was already introducing himself to me. He held out his hand. "Joe Glenn."

"Mr. Glenn, pleased to meet you, sir. Les Walker. I really like your Gerty there." And we shook hands, very grown-up.

He grinned. "Gerty likes kids, too. But not kennels. Doesn't do well in kennels. So your father said she could join you while I'm out of the country. Is that all right?"

"It sure is!"

Then Mom and Dad joined us, and they all started talking.

The other person in the van, a girl Hannah's age, swung the passenger-side door open and slid lazily down off the seat. She seemed in no hurry to do anything.

She wore makeup and had a fancy hairstyle. I recognized that it was the latest thing, the style Hannah was pestering Mom for. Mom kept saying no. This girl's mom either had said yes or was in Central America.

This girl, of course, was Lisa Glenn.

As I watched Lisa, I thought about what Bits had said. Trouble with a capital T. If so, she was sure a smooth, worldly-wise-looking piece of trouble.

Her dad reached into the back of the SUV and began unloading. And unloading. And unloading. One of the items was a stuffed polar bear. It was sitting down. If it stood up, it would have been as tall as I was and three times as wide.

Dad and I began to carry the mountain of possessions upstairs, box by box by box, suitcase by suitcase. How could one girl accumulate so much stuff?

I hoped she didn't think she was going to take all this to Minnesota on the houseboat.

We'd have to rent two of them.

3

What do you do with a mountain of stuff that won't fit in the room it's supposed to fit in? Put most of it out in the garage, of course.

Lisa didn't like that. Instead, she suggested that maybe she and the girls could trade rooms. Their superbig bedroom would hold her stuff, she insisted.

"No," said Mom.

"Yes," said Lisa.

Mom put her dainty foot down. Lisa objected. I could have told her that when Mom said something, ain't no use arguing (although I do, anyway—once in a while). I kept quiet. I figured she'd work it out.

Dad moved our van out into the driveway. Then he and I started toting stuff—from upstairs, where we had just toted it, to downstairs and out the back to the middle of the garage floor. Up and down we went. We took down everything but the laptop, TV, and clothes.

Lisa was not a happy camper. She spent the whole afternoon picking around at her stuff in the garage, carrying stuff back upstairs—stuff we had just carried down right after carrying it up.

She finally got her laptop set up by her bed, her TV arranged just so on the nightstand, her CD player plugged in and running, her deck of magazines she hadn't read yet piled beside her bed, her stack of magazines with the movie stars in them piled on the other side of her bed, and three cases of makeup and hair things laid out on the vanity. And that was for starters. There was also the suitcase full of stuffed animals for her bed, a selection of posters to cover up "that gruesome wallpaper," and stuff I couldn't identify because it went up and down and back up the stairs in shopping bags.

Our pillows weren't good enough, so she called her parents on her cell phone and told them to bring hers over. She threw her second snit of the day because the guest room wasn't wired for cable. By dinnertime, I perceived that she didn't want to be stuck in this dorky house with these dorky people for a single minute, let alone for weeks on end.

At dinner, she got into another argument with Mom. This time, she wanted to move all her stuff into the family room, so that she'd have access to cable. Mom politely said no. It went downhill from there. Finally, Dad sided with Mom, and that was the end of it.

After dinner, the girls went to their room (which, incidentally, *is* wired for cable), and I went out to the garage. I was building the world's greatest birdhouse, and there was a prize involved.

You see, when they built a new fire station

for this end of town, they turned the old one into an art center. There, for a couple bucks, you could take drawing, painting, carpentry, or woodcarving lessons. Each session ran about nine weeks at a time.

They also ran contests. Every spring was the Birdhouse Contest, with a fifty-dollar first prize. Well! I ask you: Can a master craftsman turn down a deal like that?

My birdhouse was far from done, but it was now to the point of being painted. I pried open the can of primer and nearly had a heart attack.

Because just as I lifted the lid off, Lisa Glenn, a bolt out of the blue, slammed the garage door open and screamed, "Get away from my things!"

"I'm not near your stuff!" The workbench was maybe ten feet from her pile on the garage floor.

"You were rooting through my things! You just started painting because you knew I was coming!"

"Oh, for pete's sake."

"Get out of here! And I don't want to see you in here again!"

"I'm as far away from your stuff as I can get. I'm not gonna get paint on it or anything. I don't fling paint that far."

"I said get out!"

By now I was about ready to take the can of primer and drizzle it all over her stuff. Most of the time I don't remember to pray until hours later, when it's too late. This time I remembered in time. So I prayed that she and I would both calm down.

And then I turned my back on her and started stirring the primer.

She stomped over to me. "I said, I don't want to see you in here with my things!"

"Then close your eyes." And for once, I was able to calm down even while someone was yelling at me. I was even able to think about this for a minute. "You looked out your bedroom window and saw the light on in here, right?"

"I don't want you in here!"

"I have to be in here." I wiped the paint stirrer with my brush. "We leave for Minnesota Friday, and I want the first coat on by then."

"Minnesota! Who's going to Minnesota?"

"All of us."

"You mean I'll have the whole place all to myself?"

"You're going, too." I finished my side of the birdhouse and rotated it. Primer doesn't have to go on fancy.

"Liar!"

I don't know why I stayed calm. I don't much like people calling me names that aren't true. "Suit yourself. Only if I were you, I'd have some stuff in a suitcase Friday morning early, just in case."

Her other flare-ups were nothing compared to the one she mounted now. She went storming out to confront the decision makers.

A week on a houseboat with Lisa Glenn.

I groaned.

4

"Everybody belted in?" Dad looked in his rearview mirror at us.

"Let's go," we said.

Dad pulled out onto the street. We were on our way to Minnesota.

Tiny perched right behind Mom, the best seat for watching birds and stuff along the way. Beside him sat Mike Alvarado. In the van seat behind them, Bits and my sister Catherine buried themselves in instant conversation about the next school year. Right behind Dad, Lynn and I shared a seat. That left my sister Hannah and Lisa to sit together.

Those two girls are about the same age. You would think they would prefer that arrangement instead of sitting with one of us "younger generation," as Hannah liked to put it. Nope. They instantly hated each other. At least, that's how it seemed. They didn't say three words to each other. Each one brought her own magazines, and they read them without a peep.

In the aisle by the door, curling up pretty much anywhere she wanted to, lay Gerty. She had her collar and leash, her dish, a week's worth of dog food, and a retrieving dummy. We should all travel so light.

Lisa didn't travel light anywhere, as you

may guess. Mom and Dad had to really put their foot down, or we would have filled the van to the roof. All of us but Lisa brought only one suitcase. In fact, the only extras I brought were a couple of games and a model fighter plane I was working on. It was over half done, and I was getting hot to finish it.

On the first day Dad pushed it hard, and we got way up into the top of Wisconsin on 53. He made sure that our motel had an indoor pool before he handed them his credit card. We peeled out of our clothes, into our swimsuits, and gleefully invaded the pool. Lisa chose not to participate.

Some older people gasped in shock and left, but—honest!—we weren't that rowdy. In fact, I wouldn't call us very rowdy at all. Mike was the only one who really got a stern warning from Mom: "You cannonball the guests, even accidentally, and you walk to the houseboat. Hear?"

"Yes, ma'am." And he was so afraid of walking that he quit cannonballing altogether. You see? That was the lesson Lisa was going to have to learn. Mike already knew it: You don't mess with Mom.

The next day we pulled into Duluth before noon. It would have been even earlier, but peeling Lisa out of a bed was like taking the price sticker off a glass; it just doesn't go very fast, no matter what you try.

Before we got out of the van, we each received an allowance.

Lisa declined. "Thank you, but my parents already gave me money."

"So did mine," said Tiny.

Dad smiled. "For purposes of this trip, you are all like our own children. We give our children a trip allowance—to be spent on the trip."

"Yes, but—" Lisa should have known not to argue.

"This is a gift, no strings attached. It's part of the package."

She accepted it.

We were also given to understand that there would be no additional gifts on the trip. "So spend it carefully," he said. Catherine, Hannah, and I already knew that. He just explained for benefit of the others.

We sort of looked for a tourist information center, but we didn't see one right off. There were signs to the waterfront, though, and Dad figured there must be tourist info there. It was a tourist area.

"There's an ore freighter down here somewhere," he added.

It didn't take us long to find it. But, then, how can you lose an ore freighter? The thing was a couple hundred feet long and over two stories tall. It was moored on the lakefront.

What a great boat! Ship. As we hoped, they gave tours. Dad took us kids on the tour, all through her holds and her crew quarters. Mom had toured the ore freighter before, so she stayed topside with Gerty.

I'd gone through big vessels now and then

in Seattle when we lived there, but the rest of the gang had never seen anything like it.

I mean, this ore boat was big enough to transport a couple football fields, the bleachers, the teams, and a lot of the fans. And yet, it was no longer big enough to compete with the computerized monsters that haul ore now. So here it was, a tourist attraction. It must have felt like quite a comedown to her captain.

The freighter was also very photogenic. Just ask Lynn. She was the self-appointed picture taker. She took pictures of the whole boat, many little details of the boat, and Sugar Creekers looking at it. She lined us all up around a hatch cover and got a passing tourist to take a group shot.

The last stop on the tour was one of the compartments that carried the ore (actually modified ore in the form of little iron nuggets).

Think of a big two-story house that has really high ceilings and is completely hollow. No rooms. Just one big, open, hollow box. Picture dark steel walls and very little light. No doors or windows. You enter and leave by climbing a ladder from the roof. That's the inside of just one of the compartments in that freighter.

It echoed as the guide explained the room. Then she turned and started back up the ladder toward the light of day (well, actually, toward the gift shop built on the deck up there).

Bits and I were standing by one of the iron walls. I rapped my knuckles on the wall. It sort of rang a little, like a huge, very muffled bell. We looked at each other.

We couldn't help ourselves. It was just too inviting. It was like a big, bright red lollipop to a little kid. We looked around desperately. We couldn't see anything to bang with. So Bits took off her hiking boot. She slammed it against the wall as I hollered.

Now when I really want to yell, I can call down airplanes. But I didn't have to really work at it. The huge hollow room picked up our sound and magnified it. The walls rang. I'll bet the captain of some vessel away out in the middle of the lake perked up his ears and said, "Why, that's an odd pitch for a foghorn."

My ears rang. I imagine everyone else's did too. Even the silence that followed rang. The other Creekers stood there wide-eyed, saying, "Wow!" I knew Dad would get after me, but it was worth it.

Then we scurried for the ladder. Other people were going up, so I had to pause at the bottom to wait my turn.

And for the first time, I realized something. "Hey! Where's Lisa? She's not here." As I thought about it, I couldn't remember seeing her belowdecks at all.

"She stayed up with your mother and the dog," Dad said. He did not look pleased with me. I could see that. But it wasn't like we'd disrupted the tour. The tour had just ended.

We walked outside. Mom, with Gerty on leash beside her, sat on one of the hatches. She didn't look any closer to being pleased than Dad did.

She said, "I could recognize your voice even in that echo chamber, Les! I'm ashamed of—"

But Dad interrupted. "Where's Lisa? I thought she was up here with you."

Mom looked startled. "Oh, no! I thought she was with you."

5

I thought Mom and Dad would be more upset than they were. They didn't look too worried. I sure would have been. Where had Lisa gone?

Dad said he would check the van for a note or something. He didn't think he'd find one. He supposed she'd gone looking in one of the stores.

Meanwhile, Mom led the rest of us to a great little park nearby. An old-fashioned popcorn wagon stood in the middle. So did a bezillion seagulls. So we bought popcorn to eat and to feed the birds. We took turns keeping Gerty from chasing every kernel that flew. Lynn took pictures of us feeding gulls. She also took a picture of me hanging onto Gerty.

And here I will mention something about Tiny only once. But bear in mind that he was this way the whole trip. The whole faluting trip! He whipped out his bird book and studied it. He stared at the gulls. He studied the book. Lynn took a picture of him doing it. Were these Franklin's gulls or Bonaparte's gulls? Finally he declared that these were all Franklin's gulls and therefore lifers—that is, they were a new first sighting for his life list of birds seen. He was bouncing with joy.

We were very happy for him.

But enough is enough.

I wondered where Lisa could have gone. Sure, she wasn't down in the ore boat with us. I'd finally decided she was with Mom, same as everyone else. It never ever occurred to me that she might take off without telling anyone. You just didn't do that in my family.

But she was Mom and Dad's responsibility. I just hung out and managed to have a great time in spite of Lisa.

And we Creekers *were* having a great time. In fact, not just the Gang enjoyed the day. So did my sisters, and they usually prefer malls. After popcorn time, we ran laughing along a ship canal.

We watched these really neat boats come through the locks. Seattle has a great ship canal with locks. In fact, they're right by Ballard, where we lived. Our family used to go there a lot, especially when the salmon were running. Then we could watch the wild salmon swimming up from the ocean to the lake and on up into the rivers, where they spawned.

Locks, I guess, are about the same the world over. These locks were basically walls. The water level on one side of the locks was lower than the level on the other side. The boats would sail from the lower water level through a narrow channel right up to a wall. They'd tie up. Another wall would close behind them. The place where they were between the two walls would fill with water. The wall in front of them would open, and they'd chug out into the higher water level.

Then boats from the higher side would steam into the locks. The lock would drain, and that lowered the boats to the level of the lower side. The wall would open, and out they'd go.

It was Lisa's own fault that she missed seeing all that. She was invited.

When we finally ambled back to the van, Lisa still wasn't there. Dad turned on his phone, and Mom turned on hers. Then Mom stayed at the van with us, and he went out looking.

I could tell Mom was worried now. She chewed on her lower lip a lot. She doesn't do that when she's relaxed. Also, she got out her needlepoint. Mom did a lot of handwork at odd times, like when she was waiting for the girls and me after school. She said it kept her fingers from going nuts. I'm not sure if she was serious or not. Anyway, we'd come barreling out of school and get in the car; she'd put down her sewing and drive away. It might be knitting or crocheting or cross-stitch. Right now it was needlepoint.

Over forty-five minutes later, here came Lisa from the opposite direction, in no hurry at all. She was carrying a bag of purchases. Mom called Dad to come back. Their wayward child had returned.

And so we got on the road again, an hour and some later than planned, for the last leg of our journey.

As we cruised up the highway toward Hibbing, Side Lake, and on north, I twisted in my seat to look at Lisa.

"It's hard to tell, but Mom and Dad are really mad at you, Lisa," I said softly. "I mean really mad."

"And your point is—"

Hannah interrupted. "He means that tonight you're really going to get raked over the coals. They won't embarrass you in front of the rest of us—they'll talk to you alone. But you're going to get it."

"What can they do?" Lisa smirked. "I'm too big to spank, there's no place to ground me, and they can't send me back. My parents are out of the country. So they're just going to have to live with it, now, aren't they?"

Hannah sneered. "Well, aren't you a cute piece of work!"

I turned back around in my seat and stared straight ahead, stunned. *They'll just have to live with it.* I couldn't imagine saying that about my parents—or anyone else's, for that matter!

I never could fly in the face of my folks like that.

But obviously, Lisa sure could.

6

Where I grew up in Seattle, we were used to seeing live aboards. Live aboards were those few people who owned a boat and lived on it all the time. I mean as if they didn't own a house on shore. They kept their floating home tied up on some waterway. They had hookups to electricity, phone, and sometimes sewer. So they had TV and all the latest Internet, whether or not they had a toilet that flushed. Their boats were either yachts or little one-story barges.

I was expecting our houseboat to be like that. No such thing. It was huge, with features that vacationers want. It was a flat-bottomed barge with a deck at each end. On the front deck was a really nice gas barbecue grill. On the back deck was—are you ready for this?—a sliding board into the water. The top of the board was up on the roof, and the roof was one giant sun deck with lawn chairs and a picnic table. The middle third of the sundeck was actually a closed-in upstairs bedroom. You entered it up a hatch from the kitchen.

A big inboard-outboard motor hung off the back. I mean a big one, three feet across. It caught Mike's attention instantly.

Inside, as you walked from front to back,

you passed from a living room with sofas that folded into beds on to a kitchen with a microwave, stove, and fridge. In the back were a bathroom and another bedroom. So we had all the modern conveniences.

Plus, every room except the bathroom was almost all windows. You could look out or be out. No problem.

I have mentioned before that I'm going to be a great chef when I grow up, so this was a neat opportunity. You could cook with propane gas on a regular stove, or get fancy with the grill on the deck, or zap something in a hurry in the microwave.

The best part of the opportunity was that Mom announced she was on vacation. That meant that she was not going to constantly hassle laundry or do all the cooking. She'd brought a tote bag full of books to read, so I knew she was serious.

Mom had called ahead when she saw we were going to be really late (thanks to Lisa). The people stayed up for us and even kept the dining room open! Of course, ten hungry people were a pretty good reason to keep the restaurant open a little longer. Still, it was nice of them.

Mom and Dad spent until late in the night chatting with her old schoolmate. They sent us kids down to the houseboat to get settled.

The restaurant nestled among trees a hundred yards up a slope from a big dock area. A dozen houseboats, some smaller than ours but none larger, were tied up along the pier. In deep twilight, the eight of us kids walked from the restaurant deck down to the houseboats.

Halfway down the long, sloping lawn between dining room and docks, Tiny stopped. The others went on, but I stopped with him.

"Les, this is amazing."

"It's dark. What can you still see that is amazing?"

"I mean this whole thing. My mom and dad do all right, but they're not rich. We don't take fancy vacations. In fact, my dad used to work two jobs until he got his promotion. I never dreamed I'd be able to go someplace like this. It's a gift from God."

What do you say? I couldn't think of anything.

Tiny didn't need for me to say anything. He continued, "I got to remember every day to thank Him. Remind me, will you, Les? I'm afraid I'll forget."

"Sure. And I hope He gives you lots more gifts every day."

"Yeah. So do I. And you too. Thanks." We walked on down the hill together.

Mom and Dad were going to take the bedroom, they said. That left the rest of us with only one rule: Boys upstairs, girls downstairs, work it out.

We boys solved our problems in a hurry. We unrolled sleeping bags on the carpeted upstairs floor, and that was that. Technically, it was not upstairs; it was upladder. But you know what I mean.

The girls didn't have it so easy. The sofas folded out into two double beds. Lisa figured she needed a bed to herself. But five people cramped into that downstairs place didn't permit that. One in one bed and four in the other? Uh-uh.

So she decided that Bits and Lynn ought to sleep on the floor, since they were the youngest. Besides, she said, they were not actual family members. She seemed to forget that neither was she. Want to guess how well that went over?

Surprisingly, Bits and Lynn were about ready to do it. But Hannah blew the whistle. "Absolutely not!" she insisted. "Everyone gets a bed." So she ended up sleeping with Bits and Lynn, and Lisa got stuck with Catherine.

When Lisa agreed to that arrangement, I'm sure she didn't realize that Catherine is a flopper. Bits and Lynn, Hannah reported later, slept like rocks. They stayed where laid. But Catherine flops as she sleeps. Always has, always will. She's on her left side. *Flop!* She's on her right side. *Flop!* Now she's sideways in the bed. *Flop! Flop!* All night long. Lisa had a conniption.

Gerty, bless her old heart, slept in the kitchen. She didn't seem to care what life offered; she took it all in stride. That mutt could sleep anywhere.

When I woke up the next morning, I instantly realized we had a problem. We boys were upstairs. The only bathroom was downstairs. Also, I noticed Tiny wasn't here. It took me a while to get my courage cranked up enough to open the hatch and climb down the ladder. I didn't look in the girls' direction. Then I went out to the only place I could go besides the living room—the back deck.

Tiny was sitting there with his feet dangling over the side. He had already started his day's bird list.

"Where'd you get the sketchbook? Pretty neat." I looked over his shoulder while he drew a picture. It was a great little notebook, about 6 inches by 8 inches—like a regular hardcover book, but the pages were all blank.

"Mom and Dad gave it to me. They said, 'For this trip.' I'm supposed to tell them all about it when I get back."

I watched a few minutes while he drew an island off our stern, and then turned the page and drew a houseboat like ours that was just going out. "Ever hear of a camera?"

"It's not the same thing. If I took a picture of that boat with a camera, you'd have a whole lot of water and sky and this little teeny boat way off in the distance. This way, all you see is the boat."

"That's true." I let the cool morning and the silence wrap around me. "Now explain that to Lynn."

He chuckled. "She's already used three rolls of film, and we're not even under way yet."

"Yeah, but we're very well documented."

He drew in silence, and I just sat there awhile. I liked the peace.

Then Tiny said, "I want to see a loon."

"I'd like that, too," I replied. "Did you say thank you yet?"

He grinned. "Yeah! Hey, look!"

Something flapped along low to the water, probably at least a quarter mile away. Anyhow, way off.

The grin fled. "Les, I might know birds back home. But when I get away from home, I got an awful lot to learn."

Don't we all?

7

I can't think of anyone who loves nature more than tall, lanky Tiny. So when Mom and Dad enslaved us to help haul groceries aboard the houseboat, and he got sidetracked by a small brown bird hiding in a bush, nobody said anything. We all knew he pulled his weight and then some. As responsibility goes, he was an adult.

It was a different story with Lisa. She managed to get out of doing any work at all, and I don't know how she did it. She didn't stand still. She didn't just sit. And yet, she did not carry a solitary thing aboard. Not even a can of tuna.

At first, I wondered if Mom even noticed. Then I decided she hadn't. She didn't say anything.

We unloaded the coolers into the refrigerator. We filled it so full I stacked things two and three deep. But then, when it's a little refrigerator and a big mob, what would you expect? We filled the closet next to the fridge with canned stuff—chicken for one night's main meal, stew for another, fruit cocktail for breakfast and snacks.

And we had lots of real snack stuff, too. Junk food. Whatever you want to call nuts, cheese puffs, pretzels, popcorn, and three kinds of chips. A couple cases of soft drinks topped it off. Mom had decided that vacation is vacation and that we wouldn't die if we ate stuff that wasn't nutritious for one week out of the year. The other fifty-one weeks, of course, she was death on soft drinks and junk food. It must have been really hard on her to watch her only son, the baby of the family, pop the top on a Pepsi with so much enthusiasm.

We double-checked the van for stuff that might have been left under the seats or somewhere. Dad parked it up behind the boathouse in a long-term lot. The semigrown-ups and grown-ups bought fishing licenses in the little convenience store there.

The girls set up a banquet of snack food on the roof and settled into those deck chairs.

Dad torched off that huge engine.

Mom cast off the mooring lines.

We were on our way, adventuring!

Dad pulled down a radio mike from a hook overhead. It squawked. He reached down and adjusted something by turning a knob on the set near the floor. He announced to someone that we were headed for such-and-so campsite on Mitchell Island. I think it was Mitchell. Anyway, he told someone where we were going.

A disembodied voice acknowledged him.

So we had radio. Real ship-to-shore radio, even if shore was two hundred feet away! How great! We purred out into the main body of water.

What a glorious ride! Small forested islands

drifted by on each side of us. We'd chug out into a broad place—either a large pond or a small lake, whatever you prefer to call it—and cross it. Then we'd enter another narrow passage. Silence, except for the huge Johnson inboard-outboard. Peace.

You can control the boat from inside in the living room or from outside up on the roof. So Dad called Tiny to take the controls while he came upladder and sat himself at the rooftop wheel. Then he took over steering again while Mom navigated.

Mike was green with envy of Tiny.

I hung off the rail and imagined coming through here a hundred eighty years ago. One of the voyageurs. For fifty minutes of every hour you paddled like crazy, driving a long freight canoe made of birchbark through the lakes. All day, for weeks at a time, you worked. Each night, you started a fire, cooked your meal, and ate it. And in your spare time, you patched leaks in the canoes.

The lakes were not always connected the way these waterways were. When you hit a place where the canoe couldn't go, you had to carry everything from there to the next lake, sometimes for miles. "Portaging," it was called. You took everything out of the boat. You carried the heavy canoe from point to point. You carried all the freight—which was wrapped in eighty-pound bundles—and you stowed it back into the canoes at the other end. If it was a short portage, the men might carry two packs each—a hundred sixty pounds! What a hard life! Yet the voyageurs lived like this, hauling millions of dollars in furs out of the wilderness, taking tons of supplies back in.

We passed a little log cabin at water's edge. The only way to get there was by boat; it was on an island. Catherine daydreamed out loud about living somewhere like that. She kept figuring out ways to get cable television out there, because she couldn't imagine not having TV. Dad said satellite TV was the wave of the future.

Mike explained how you can get e-mail by cell phone. Dad said that was the wave of the future.

Hannah said she couldn't wait for everyday e-mail shopping—like for groceries and underwear—to become practical. Then she'd just buy all her stuff over the Web. They'd bring her order in a helicopter and drop it off at the door, and she could live anywhere. Dad said that was the wave of the future.

The future sure has a lot of waves.

I could not picture a voyageur with e-mail.

Lynn stepped in front of me and aimed her camera. "Smile."

I smiled. *Click*. "Lynn girl, you're gonna run out of film by two o'clock tomorrow."

"I brought twelve rolls from home and bought six more in Duluth."

"I know."

"Pessimist," she said. And she disappeared down the ladder to the lower deck, I suppose to take more pictures of something.

I kind of dreamed, half-awake and half in some other universe. Voyageurs and Northwest Company men (the American version of the British/Canadian freight haulers) paddled in and out of my thoughts. And then I got snapped back to reality.

Lisa was tapping me on the shoulder. She dipped her head, a come-with-me gesture. I followed her down the ladder to the main deck.

She kept her voice low. "I looked everywhere, and I can't find it. Where does your dad hide the beer?"

8

"I'm dying for a cigarette."

Lisa wandered out onto the back deck, so I followed her. She flopped down in a chair. I flopped down in the other one, just to be sociable. Besides, I was tired of hearing how Catherine was going to live in lovely isolation with all the conveniences of the city.

A flat, frothy wake like a silver ribbon churned out behind us. We weren't raising many waves at all.

I told her, "I think Dad keeps his cigarettes in the same place where he keeps his beer—he doesn't use either of them."

"Everybody drinks beer. Maybe he's just cutting back for a week."

I shrugged. Why argue? I'd lived with the man all my eleven years. Now here was this girl, who knew him three days so far, telling me about his personal life. Go figure.

I watched a seagull flap its way stiffly across the pond. I hoped that Tiny saw it, too. "Sorry about the beer. And the cigarettes."

"Oh, I have the cigarettes. I just figured there'd be some beer aboard, you know?"

"No, I don't know. I never thought of it."

"That's 'cause you're just a little kid yet." She glanced at me. "You're a kinda cute little kid—the red hair and freckles. Is that really your hair color?"

"Who in their right mind would deliberately dye it this color?"

She giggled.

Actually, there was another reason I sat down there talking to Miss Worldly.

The chairs were now out of the shade, and it was really sunny up on the top deck. I'd started to feel it. My face and neck were getting hot, and I just knew that any minute I'd turn lobster red up there. Kids with freckles don't take the sun very well.

And, frankly . . . well . . . uh . . . I forgot my hat. Totally forgot. I packed a million things, unpacked half of them, and packed half a million other things, but my hat was still hanging in my closet back home.

I sure didn't tell Lisa that, of course. If I was really lucky, she wouldn't notice. I was hoping that Mom or Dad wouldn't notice either.

What kind of small talk do you make with a girl like Lisa? "So where'd you get the cigarettes? Bring them from home?"

She shook her head. "Dad confiscated mine. I should have hid them better. So I restocked in Duluth."

She said it so matter-of-factly, as if it was the easiest thing to walk up to the counter and buy a pack. I knew better than that. There are laws against selling cigarettes to kids.

The motor cut to half-speed. It rumbled,

not working much at all. Our wake settled farther until there was hardly any there.

Dad came bouncing down the aft ladder. "Oh, there you are." He continued inside.

I got up and followed him. He settled onto the tall seat at the console. He cut the motor down more. He turned the wheel, trying to watch all sides at once. "Get the port mooring line, Les."

Port. That was left. I pushed the big glass sliding door open and stepped out onto the front deck. We were ten feet from a curved, sandy beach. Gerty's thick, heavy tail was wagging wildly.

The only real decks were fore and aft. Along the sides were strips of deck about six inches wide; just barely wide enough for your foot. I climbed out onto that narrow strip along the left (excuse me, *port*) side of the boat.

The boat waggled a little and almost tossed me into the drink. Then it growled to a stop, its blunt nose jammed into the beach sand.

Gerty barked excitedly, but I couldn't think of anything she was barking at. Maybe she was not a sea dog and was just that glad to see land.

I found the mooring line. There it was, a really thick rope lying in long, loose loops on this narrow side deck. But what did I do with it? Where was I supposed to moor it?

Mom came out through the sliding glass door. She opened up the railing in the very front, which was actually a gate, and jumped down into the water. She waded ashore.

"Toss it to me!" She raised her arms, waiting.

I flung it as hard as I could, and it almost got to her. She waded out, retrieved the end, and dragged it ashore. She tied it to a big metal ring set in a rock. I hadn't noticed it. The rope stretched so taut it was starting to drag the beached boat sideways.

But she hurried to the starboard (the right) side as Mike threw her the other mooring line. She tied it off on another ring.

Bound fast with a heavy line sticking out each side, the boat was going nowhere. Dad shut down the engine.

Then Mom waded back out to the very nose of the boat, clunked around there a moment, and dragged a gangplank out onto the sand. So that was how you tie up at a camp spot for the night. Next time, I'd be more help, I promised myself.

Mom came aboard via the gangplank. "Les, I brought a bag of avocados from home that ought to be used today. You make the appetizer, please."

"Aw right!" Something I could do!

I could do it because I'd done it before. And if you don't mind my saying so, it always turned out great. While Dad started the grill on the front deck, and Mom got out the frozen microwave french fries, and Hannah ripped up lettuce for the salads, I started the appetizer.

The secret (this is a future great chef speaking) is in the vinegar. For this dish, you use rice vinegar. Either plain or seasoned works fine. Rice vinegar has a very gentle, rich flavor, much more so than does plain old cheap vinegar.

In a glass salad-dressing bottle I mixed two-thirds salad oil and one-third rice vinegar. That was it.

Dad started steaks. I chopped tomatoes for Hannah. Mom did the fries. Catherine set out the flatware, paper plates, and paper salad bowls. I copped another ten salad bowls. In each I cut an avocado in half and removed the stone. I shook the oil and vinegar mixture very well and drizzled it over the two halves in each dish. I set the bowls on the plates, one at each place. Catherine put out the napkins. The table looked pretty elegant.

Dad came in long enough to say grace with us and get his appetizer. Then he minded the grill out on the deck while we ate our first course, the avocados. Incidentally, part of the reason he stayed outside with the steaks was Gerty. She took an intense interest in them.

We were done with the appetizer by the time the steaks were ready. Well, sort of done. I think Bits ate hers only to be polite. She didn't seem to appreciate it the way Lynn and Mike and all of us Walkers did.

Lisa apparently voted to go ahead and be impolite.

She didn't even touch hers.

Oh well. Her loss.

But it hurt me a little, all the same.

9

I've always secretly suspected that french fries are not a vegetable product. Lisa Glenn confirmed it for me.

Think about it. A person who really enjoys meat often eats french fries with his steak or barbecued pork or hamburger or whatever. I'd eat nothing but meat if Mom would let me, but I'd eat fries, too. I love fries. See? So fries can't be a vegetable.

Lisa did not touch my avocado. She did not even nibble at her salad. She devoured her steak, though. And she ate her fries. Proof positive that there's something animal about fries. And an avocado isn't your average veggie, either. It's as close to meat as you can get without butchering something.

Here's more proof. Gerty lay down near the table. Not under it, where the begging would be too obvious, but near it. When some salad lettuce fell on the floor, Gerty didn't bother to get up. But when a french fry fell, she was on it like a hawk on a mouse.

During dinner, Tiny crowed about all the birds he had seen that day. Hannah and Catherine loved the islands and the solitude (which surprised me—weren't these the same two who were talking about e-groceries and satellite TV?).

Lynn had done lots of things, some of them in foreign countries. But she'd never done anything like this, she said. She was glowing.

Bits babbled on about something, but I don't remember what. Mike loved the boat and looked forward to what he thought was his divine right to get to pilot it sooner or later.

And Lisa? She pouted. She answered curtly when Mom or Dad asked something. She didn't respond at all when one of us lesser beings spoke to her. She didn't complain about any one thing. She just made sure we knew that the world was a mess, her part of it in particular, and it was all our fault.

After supper, we all trooped off the boat. Gerty decided she was not a gangplank-walking dog and jumped over the side. She swam ashore. Then she spent the rest of the evening sticking her nose in every bush and log on the site.

We human beings took chairs with us. On a little outcrop to the left (that's *port*, remember), a rocky point, a fire ring had been built. It was the ring-of-rocks kind that you sit around at camp. We got a roaring blaze going in it and made s'mores.

All you campers know what s'mores are. Over the fire, you toast a marshmallow just right. Not burnt and not too light. Brown and puffy. Next, you lay a piece of chocolate bar on a graham cracker square and put the hot marshmallow on top of that. Clap another cracker piece on top of it, and you have a pure sugar sandwich.

So here we sat on our first night of the week, tied up on a tiny island in the middle of a very large national park. We ate delicious dessert while the sun coasted low beyond the island.

Finally, Mom sat back in her chair and looked from face to face. "You people did very well with dinner tonight! Thank you all. Hannah, Catherine, Les, tomorrow evening you don't have to do anything. Mike and Lynn, will you do the cooking tomorrow? And Tiny?"

"Sure!" Mike grinned. "You want enchiladas? I make rocket-fuel enchiladas!"

Mom smiled. "I was thinking more along the line of Chinese. We have canned chow mein in there and frozen cooked pork. Lynn, if you'll do the salad, and Tiny, if you will set the table and clear it afterward, we'll have it."

They were grinning as widely as Mike. Even Tiny. But then, he never seemed to mind dirty work.

Mom turned to Lisa. "I couldn't help but notice, Lisa, that you didn't take part in any of the work today. None of it. So you can do the dishes tonight and tomorrow. The person who does the dishes also cleans up the kitchen and puts things away."

Did I say snit? Try rage. Lisa glared at Mom, furious almost beyond words. "Somebody will have to help me."

"You won't need help. There isn't much

tonight. Flatware, mostly, and the salad mixing bowl."

"There's a dishwasher on this tub, right?"

"Right. You."

Lisa was so angry she choked her words out. "That's very funny. But you can't make me. You're not my mom."

"Excuse me a moment." Mom got up and walked down to the houseboat.

Dad said quietly, "Lisa, are you familiar with the legal term *in loco parentis*?"

She didn't say anything, but she looked at him.

"It means," he explained, "'in place of the parent.' Your father and I worked out the legally binding documents and filed them. He signed over his parental rights to us until he returns. And Mrs. Walker and I signed the necessary papers to accept responsibility for you with all the rights of a parent. This way, for instance, if you should get sick or you're injured, we can give permission for medical treatment just as your parents would."

Dad paused because Mom was coming back. She carried a brown bag with some sort of gift-shop logo on it. It was too dark to see well.

"I have a gift for you, Lisa."

Lisa frowned.

Mom handed her the bag and sat down again.

Lisa peeked in it. The frown deepened. She brought out a small book. It looked kind of like

Tiny's sketchbook. But his had a plain cover. Hers had flowers on it. When she opened it, I could see that the pages were lined but blank. With it were a couple of really neat-looking ballpoint pens.

"It's a journal," Mom explained. "In it you write down your thoughts, whatever they are at the moment. Not just what you did in a day, but why you did it, what you felt while you were doing it . . ."

"This is punishment for going shopping in Duluth?"

"No, at the time I bought it for you, I still thought you were with the others. I got it at a gift shop across from the ore freighter. You are a girl with very strong feelings. That's good. But I'm not sure you yourself know what they are. Journaling is a way to find out. Also, it's a lot of fun."

"I don't want to."

"You don't have to. But I did want to let you know that there is such a thing as journaling. And that it's helpful."

"What do you care?"

"That's what I've just been explaining, Lisa," Dad said. "We care because for the moment we are *in loco parentis*. Standing in for your parents."

"That also means," he continued, "that we treat you neither better nor worse than we treat our own children. For the moment, you're a member of our family. Our kids accept responsibility as family members. We expect it from you also."

And then Dad's voice took on a hard edge. I don't know if Lisa recognized it, but I sure did. It didn't happen often, thank goodness. But it was happening now. He was no longer the kindly lawyer explaining a law term. He was laying down the law. And he sounded danger-ous. "So, when we tell you to do something, you will do it."

Lisa jumped up and stomped off to the houseboat. She marched up the gangplank and slammed inside through the glass sliding door. I'm surprised that she didn't break it, she was so rough.

As I mentioned, the boat's walls were nearly all window. You could see her inside as she flopped onto a sofa and sulked big time.

Did she take her new journal in along with her? Yes, she did. I didn't see her get it out and write in it, but she didn't leave it behind. If I was that mad, I think I wouldn't have accepted it.

No one said anything. The other Sugar Creekers had recognized that hard tone of voice, too. Here around the campfire, things were really heavy.

The lake turned gold. Suddenly Tiny jumped to his feet and ran down to the water's edge, out to the very tip of the point.

Mostly out of curiosity, I walked down and stood beside him. Gerty came, too. I think it was because she hadn't gotten that part of the site completely sniffed yet.

"Listen!" Tiny was gazing out across the golden water, his head cocked slightly.

Away out on the lake somewhere, someone laughed. And laughed again. It was an eerie sound and fascinating. I can't describe it. It sounded almost like a jungle movie.

"It's a loon," he said, a wee bit gravel voiced. "A real loon. I just heard a loon."

On his face was a rapt look of happiness.

And in his eyes were tears of joy.

10

S wim time!

Well, OK, so it wasn't exactly the warmest weather. But the light overcast would burn off by the time we got back out of the water. We tossed a bucket of water on the big blue slide to make it slick.

Mom grinned. "Cannonball your heart out, Mike!"

"Oh, yeah!" Gleefully, Mike jogged up the ladder, out onto the top deck, and zoomed down the slide.

And I was right behind him!

Mike swooped down the slide and straight out the bottom. He tucked into a ball and hit the water with enough swoosh to soak Minneapolis. What a great cannonball!

And he surfaced with the loudest earsplitting scream I've ever heard.

"A-a-a-a-a-a-i-i-i-i-i-e-e-e-e-e!"

But I was on the lip of the slide and headed down before my brain decided what his scream might mean. *Maybe the water is not quite as warm as I'm hoping.*

That was a correct interpretation.

I hit the water. And died. Died, I tell you! Never—never!—in my young life had I ever jumped into water that cold.

I surfaced screaming, just as Mike had.

Everyone on the back deck of the boat was laughing like crazy at us.

But not Lisa. She was still in bed.

I heard about something weeks later, but I'll tell you about it here, because at this point was when it happened. It's easiest to keep the story in the right order of time.

What happened was this:

The night before, the fire died down, and everyone went to bed. Lisa started to get ready for bed, too.

Mom said, "No, you have to clean up the kitchen yet."

"I'll do it tomorrow." Lisa brushed her teeth.

Mom was waiting for her when she came out of the bathroom. "Tonight."

Lisa started to push past her.

Mom turned her around suddenly, and she was facing the sink. "You'll complete your work. There's not that much of it."

And Lisa decided she was not going to.

Mom stayed up, waiting.

Lisa stayed up, trying to outwait her.

At 2:00 A.M., Mom got too sleepy and called Dad. So he got up to keep Lisa awake until she did her chore.

When I first heard that, I thought, *Man, is that cruel!* But as I thought more about it, I could see it wasn't. Her whole life long, Lisa was going to have to do things she didn't want to do. She would have to take orders from a lot

53

of people—bosses, teachers, police officers, maybe even a judge. On top of that, she had to learn to get along in a group.

Finally, apparently around 4:00, Dad asked, "What is it you want, Lisa? Talk about it."

It took her awhile, but she finally started talking. "I want out of here, that's what I want! Minnesota, of all places! What a bunch of hicks! We might as well be stuck in Oklahoma." And on and on she went.

Dad nodded. "I grew up on a farm. I was a hick. And I loved it. It never occurred to me that you might think differently. I'm sorry you have to go through this." And by the time he was done sweet-talking her, she had the kitchen cleaned up and they both could finally get to bed.

Dad can alter his voice to suit any occasion. I have heard him speak in public, and he sounds convincing. And loud. When he talks to the girls or me, he can sweet-talk or demand, but it's always the right tone of voice for the occasion. That night, he had Lisa buying everything he said, just with his tone of voice. It's a gift.

Mom doesn't have that gift. She has other gifts.

And a long time later, Mom admitted to me, "If your dad hadn't taken over, Lisa would have had me. I was about to give up. She would have won the power struggle."

Anyway, that's why Lisa was still sleeping

while we had breakfast on the roof deck. And then we tried this swimming adventure.

The boys and Dad all went swimming then. Bits jumped right in, and Lynn eased her way in—once. That was enough. Mom got conned into it. Hannah and Catherine decided not to. Nobody made them.

And Gerty. Dear old Gerty. You'd think a black Lab would be born to it. She saw us all in the water, and she so wanted to go in. But she'd had enough of cold water just getting from the boat to land without using the gangplank. So she made herself a nervous wreck. But she didn't get wet.

"It's only cold down deep." Bits sculled along on her back. "The top three inches aren't too bad."

"Yeah," I groused. "But my body is more than three inches deep." I didn't spend a whole lot of time just swimming. Gerty had a good idea there. Going down the slide was fun, though, and I did it many times.

Lisa showed her face around noon, just in time for lunch.

Even though the day was overcast, it was warm enough that we all ate lunch up on the top deck. Mom had made brownies at home and secretly brought them aboard, disguised in a plain bag. She popped them out now. We all cheered.

After lunch, Dad went ashore fishing. He claimed nothing bites in the afternoon, but he went anyway. Mike and the girls went with him.

I was going too, but Mom said, "Les?"

I turned around and went back to her.

"Do you know where Lisa is?"

"No. But she can't go far. This is an island."

"Still, it's pretty easy to get disoriented. The woods are thick. You can't see far."

"I'll go back the trail a little way."

"Take Tiny, if he doesn't mind."

"Why? You think I'll get lost, too?"

She smirked. "Not you, Christopher Columbus. Ask him anyway, please."

That's why, a couple minutes later, here went Tiny and I out along a lakeside trail. When I asked him, he seemed eager to go back the trail. Overeager, in fact.

I asked him, "What are you looking for?"

"Nothing. Everything. This is so neat, Les."

We walked with the gurgling lakeshore on our right and silent forest on our left. The water lapped in among the rocks. It splashed them and kept them wet. It made muddy little minibeaches only a foot or so wide. The lake looked bright even without full sun.

On our left, the woods pressed against us, very dark. The trees and brush covering this little island hid thousands of creatures, I was sure. But nothing moved. No sound, no smell, no sight of anything told us what might be hiding in there.

Tiny stopped to make a sketch of a weird tree fungus. I borrowed his binoculars while he drew. I didn't see anything.

Then the woods came to life. Actually, it

was only Gerty. She came romping up the trail to us. And a hundred feet behind her, here came Lisa. Gerty smelled like wet dog. Lisa smelled like cigarette smoke.

Lisa wrinkled her nose. "What are you guys doing way out here?" She looked at Tiny's sketchbook. "Tiny, that is so dorky. Ooh, and colored pencils! The other first graders will be so jealous."

"My mom and dad gave it to me for this trip, so I gotta use it."

She held out her hand, so he gave it to her.

Beside her shoulder, I could see as she thumbed through it. Tiny drew wonderful pictures. Yesterday we had seen a dragonfly just coming out of its nymph skin. The nymph— pre-adult—is big, clumsy looking, and has tiny eyes. No wings. The stiff-as-cardboard skin, shaped exactly like a young dragonfly, clung to a log a foot above the water. The back had split open, and this adult dragonfly had squeezed about halfway out of the skin. Its wings were tiny shriveled lumps, not expanded yet. And Tiny had drawn it perfectly.

Here was a picture of a snoozing heron, perched on one long leg, with its neck scrunched down. Here was a whole page of wildflowers. Another page was nothing but brown wood-nymph butterflies.

"So you did all this because your parents told you to. Tell you what. Now you don't have to." She suddenly tossed the sketchbook toward the lake!

Then she took off at a run, laughing, but we didn't chase her. Tiny and I both yelled. I dived after the book. It lodged between two big rocks, less than an inch above the water. I splashed in, shoes and all, and grabbed it. I could just see the wind sending it the rest of the way into the lake.

It was dirty and a couple pages were bent, but it wasn't wet. Thank you, Lord! I handed it to Tiny.

He wagged his head. "That girl's crazy!"

And gutsy, I thought—Tiny was bigger than she was. But I didn't say that to him. He was mad enough as it was.

We walked back to the houseboat. In all that way, we heard only one bird.

Tiny frowned. "Hermit thrush?"

I shrugged. "I only know two bird calls. Crow and not-a-crow. That's not-a-crow."

He laughed, and it lightened his mood some.

When we got to the boat, though, no one was laughing.

Dad looked at me grimly. "There's a change of plans. Catherine is sick."

11

Catherine was too big to curl up in Mom's lap. She curled up there anyway, looking miserable. She didn't get sick much, but when she did, it really floored her. We gathered on the roof deck for a council of war.

Dad said, "I phoned the houseboat rental company and told them about our problem. They said, instead of us bringing the houseboat back, they'll send out a speedboat. It's on its way. Catherine's mother will take her down to Hibbing. There's a medical clinic there. Les, I want you to go along. If your mother needs something, you can be her legs. Help her carry things. And, Lisa, I want you to go with them, too, please."

She shrugged ever so casually. But I thought I could see a smug, happy smirk in there somewhere. A little rural hick town is better than no town at all.

"What'll the rest of us do?" Lynn asked.

"Stay here. Go fishing. Play games. Swim. Wait," Dad replied. "I'll stay here with you."

I heard a boat motor way, way off in the distance. "I bet that's our ride."

Dad nodded. "Probably. Lisa and Les, take your toothbrushes and a set of clean underwear. You'll almost certainly be gone overnight."

Lisa and I jogged down the ladder and ran inside. I jogged right back up the other little ladder into the guys' bedroom. I got my toilet kit and underwear, and I got clean socks, too. The ones I had on were squishy wet from jumping in the lake after that sketchbook. I figured I'd change them in the car. I put everything in the little sack that usually held my sleeping bag.

What else would I need? What if I went out to get something for Mom because she was busy? I'd better take money. I stuffed my trip allowance into the bag.

As I carried the sack out onto the back deck, a powerboat pulled alongside. Man, those guys could really operate a boat! They came roaring up. At the exact right moment they cut the motor, and their boat drifted gently against ours.

They were only a couple years older than I was, too. I'm sure at least one of them was too young to get a driver's license. They looked so casual, as if there was nothing to handling a boat. They wore shower thongs, T-shirts, cut-offs, and ball caps. You can't get much more casual than that.

One held the two boats together securely. The other helped Mom and Catherine aboard. Lisa and I climbed in. Lisa grabbed the last open seat, but that was no problem. I just sat on the floor—I mean, deck.

They pushed off and gunned it. We roared away. I waved good-bye to Dad and the others.

They were all lined up against the top rail, waving back. Down on the back deck, Gerty moved her tail back and forth, as if unsure whether she should wag it or not.

The houseboat had been fun. We chugged along and really saw the scenery. But this powerboat was *lots* of fun! The boy operating it got it up on plane, its nose pointed high. We howled along, raising a huge wake behind us. It was much too noisy to talk or hear.

We skimmed between little islands I was sure I had never seen. And those two boatmen didn't need a map.

Here was something I had never thought about before. This country was totally strange to me. I could get lost in a heartbeat here. It all looked alike to me, because this was my first time in it.

These two boys grew up here. They knew all the routes and shortcuts. They knew who lived in the houses along the shore. Well, most of them, at least. They got around here the way I could get around in my neighborhood. This was their neighborhood. The only real difference was that I prowled mine on a bike and they rode around theirs in a whizzing boat.

A seaplane came in low over our heads and landed in the water behind us. These boys probably knew the owner of that plane.

We arrived at the company dock in just a few minutes. It's amazing how quickly that powerboat made the trip, and how slowly the houseboat moved.

Mom thanked them and offered them a tip. They refused it. One of them ran (I mean, he ran literally) up to the long-term parking lot beyond the boathouse and brought our van down to us.

Mom and Catherine buckled up in the front seat; Lisa and I climbed into a backseat. Mom took off down the road.

When I thought about it, I realized that Mom was home here, too, the same as those young men. She grew up near here. She had come up into Voyageurs often. She knew the way to Hibbing without a map.

I got my socks changed. My running shoes were still wet, but the dry socks helped a lot. At least they didn't squish.

We arrived in town around 3:30. Mom turned left at the stoplight, arched around through an alley, and turned into the clinic parking lot. We all got out.

Catherine had a fever line across her lips now, and her face was red. It does that first thing when she's fevered. Mom looked worried. We all trooped into the waiting room.

Lisa plunked down in a chair. She had assumed her classic pout again, obviously displeased with life. What was cranking her this time I had no idea. She hadn't said a single word the whole trip in. She crossed her arms tightly in front of her and smoldered.

Half a dozen people were sitting around in chairs. Some thumbed through magazines or a newspaper. One older lady was crocheting a doily. Two watched fussy little kids.

Mom talked to the receptionist while I looked at magazine dates. That's something Dad tipped me off to. "See how outdated the mags are," he said. "You might be surprised."

I found one that was almost two years old.

Mom came over to us. "They're crowded and running behind. This is going to take awhile. Why don't you two get out and move around a little and come back in an hour or so?" She added plaintively, "But don't get lost."

"Lost? Me?" I cried out indignantly. "Les Columbus?"

"Columbus got lost."

"Well, he would've got where he wanted to go if that spare continent hadn't been in the way."

Mom smiled. She kissed me a quick peck on the forehead. She didn't see Lisa, but I did.

Lisa was rolling her eyes ceilingward in disgust.

12

This town—" Lisa added an expression I won't bother you with.

We stood on a street corner—one of the few in Hibbing, I might add. It's a small town and simple.

"What's wrong with it?" I asked.

"What's right with it?" she responded.

"It could be a mile north of here, where there's no buildings at all."

She rolled her eyes again. Then, "Oh—ma'am?" she shouted. "Ma'am!" She hurried catty-corner across the street to a rather portly woman walking along the other side.

I had to hurry to catch up.

Lisa asked the woman, "We're strangers here. Which way is the mall, please?"

All smiles, the woman pointed. "Go up to that four-way stop and turn left. Two blocks that way. You'll see it near the light."

"Thank you, ma'am." Lisa took off practically at a jog.

I wondered what she was so anxious to get to. Maybe she was just hungry to go shopping.

"I didn't *think* the place could be this small." She marched on. Pretty soon, she added, "And it was just plain nasty of your mom to refuse to give me any money."

"You asked nicely, too." I recalled Lisa's behavior at the doctor's office. It was like you threw a switch. She was ugly one moment and smiling and wheedling the next. Instant change.

"She doesn't need cash," Lisa whined. "She has plastic. She could pay the doctor and pharmacist with a credit card. It's not fair!"

We turned at the four-way stop as the woman had instructed. When she told us two blocks, she was talking about mighty long blocks. We walked and walked and walked.

Lisa started to flag. "This dump of a place doesn't even have a cab!"

"What would you pay the fare with, Lisa?"

"You have money. You could."

"Not a chance. I spend my money on good stuff." I glanced at her face and added, "It's only two blocks. You'll make it fine."

"The mall I really want to go to is Mall of America. Maybe we can talk your father into going there on the way back. We went right past it, I'm sure."

"Mom and Dad don't do malls, as a rule. It's not that you didn't try on our way up."

Boy, did she! She must have spent four hours trying to talk Dad into the side trip.

"Hey!" I crowed. "Here we are!"

The mall in Hibbing, it turned out, was a strip mall with maybe half a dozen businesses. All the stores fronted onto the main highway. A lot of malls have women's clothing stores and fancy gift shops. This one started out with a hardware store at this end. Way cool! I love hardware stores.

But Lisa had stopped dead in her tracks. "This is it?" She stood aghast. "This is the mall?"

"What's the matter with it? It's a great mall! Look! A hardware store and a—"

"I can't believe it! In a real mall, the anchor store is upscale! You know—a nice department store!"

"What's an anchor store?"

She looked at me as if I'd just eaten earthworms. "An anchor store is the big one on the end. Or maybe there are two with a Sears in the middle. Or Bloomingdale's. You know what I mean. This mall's end store is a *snowmobile dealer!*"

"So? We could go look at snowmobiles."

"Oh, don't be so totally dorky." She wandered along, completely dejected. "You are such a hopeless case."

The mall also had a very small drugstore and a florist shop.

"We could go in there and look at carnations," I suggested, pointing to the flower shop.

She gave me a withering glare.

"OK, let's see what's in the drugstore. Maybe there's some food."

"Look!" She poked a finger at my face. "I am the leader. You are the follower. You got that? And if you ever want to be anything other than a nerdy religious freak, you'd better start paying attention!" She wheeled and marched away—right into the drugstore.

Believe it or not, they had a little soda counter. "I'll buy you a snack," I offered. I almost called her "peerless leader," but I didn't. She was ticked off enough already.

We got malts and donuts.

It would have been nice if she had said thank you. But she didn't.

That wasn't the half of it, though. On the way out, we passed the cosmetics aisle. I the follower walked on by. Cosmetics aisles are a big step lower than underwear aisles, and I hate shopping for underwear! Lisa the leader fell to studying the rows and rows of goodies. I use the term *goody* very loosely.

"Les, loan me seven dollars."

"Sorry."

"I know you have it. I saw your money when you paid for the malts and donuts. I'll pay you back."

"When? You're out of money and no hope of getting any more."

She looked at me. "Les." She used the tone of voice Mom would use on a two-year-old. "I'll pay you back."

"Sorry."

She turned on the instant anger. That girl's on-off switch was amazing. "What is the matter with you?! A simple loan, and you act like a little baby with a piggy bank." She gave her voice a sarcastic whine. "It's m-i-i-ine."

"Lisa, my folks have a tight rule. One of the tightest. You don't spend beyond your allowance. Period. Not ever. You want something, you save up for it. And when the money's gone, you're done spending."

"That has nothing to do with this."

"Sure it does." I wasn't sure how to explain it, though. "It must be pretty important if they're so hot on it. And I do what they say. I honor their rules."

Lisa was really mad, but now she hid it so you could hardly see it. There went those eyes rolling ceilingward again. "Let me point out the obvious here—*they aren't going to know.*"

Again, what I wanted to say didn't come out nearly as smoothly as I wished. "It doesn't matter if they do or not. I'm going to do what they want."

She called me a name polite folks just don't call other people and added, "You are such a cheap, selfish—"

I couldn't think of anything to say, so I just said, "Sorry."

She waved a card with a lipstick in a plastic bubble on it. "Seven dollars! It's nothing!" She glared at me for a moment longer, so furious she could have toasted marshmallows. "You and your parents are phonies! All this praying at meals and in the morning! You aren't Christians! Christians are faith, hope, and charity. If you were a Christian, you'd show some charity!"

Right there I should have had some Bible argument for her, because I knew there must be one. I just couldn't think of any. She was badmouthing my parents, and I couldn't think of a comeback!

And then she tossed in a little bad-mouthing toward Jesus and God, too. *It's just a tube of lipstick,* I thought. She could write down the color name and get some when she got back home if she wanted. Somehow, it had become a cause to fight for, and I couldn't understand why.

Anyway, I didn't fight.

She explained again how I wasn't really a Christian or I'd buy it for her. She ended up throwing it on the floor and storming out.

I felt like a hole in the ground. But she was the leader, and I was the follower, so I followed.

As I passed the checkout counter by the door, the man at the cash register said, "Hey, kid? Tell Miss Congeniality there that it's a good thing she didn't try to lift it."

"You mean steal it?"

"Shoplift it. Yeah. I watched you on the video monitor. You'd be talking to the cops now, if she had."

"I'll tell her." I went on outside, about as embarrassed as a kid can get.

But not, I hasten to add, as embarrassed as I would have been if I'd gotten arrested.

Where was she? I didn't see her. Oh. There she was, marching up the street.

In the wrong direction.

13

This town," Lisa Glenn, worldly philosopher, announced to the world, "is the total absolute pits! It can't get any pits-er!"

I thought it had a pretty nice little park here. I wouldn't say it out loud, though, because she was still so mad. We sat on a bench because Lisa was, as the small-town hicks say, plumb tuckered out.

We had walked four or five blocks before she realized she hadn't seen a solitary one of these houses ever before. No familiar landmarks. So she turned down a small street and went a few blocks farther. Then she turned again. When we came to this park, she plopped onto the bench instantly.

On a bench twenty feet away, a really old man with a cane was feeding stuff to birds. He was tossing things from a brown paper bag. Bread chunks, it looked like.

Besides the regular brown birds you usually see in town, he had a crow and some gulls strutting around in front of him. He also had a pair of mallard ducks, so there must have been water somewhere close by. Oh, and squirrels. He was feeding squirrels, too.

It was a neat sight. He was so gentle and slow. No, not slow. Leisurely. And nothing seemed the least bit afraid of him. They were probably all old friends.

I don't think Lisa noticed. An old man feeding things was probably way too dorky for her.

"Will you quit swinging your feet!" she snapped.

I quit.

"You're constantly moving. You just have to be doing something all the time, don't you! Why can't you just sit still for once?"

I shrugged. "I'm sitting."

"But not still!"

"Sorry."

"And quit saying you're sorry every other word! I'm sick of hearing it."

I looked at her face, at her eyes. I was expecting anger, and anger was there. But something else was there, too. Was I seeing fear? Was the great peerless leader afraid of something?

She scowled. "And quit staring at me. You're acting like you're at the circus sideshow."

"Yeah, but at least I'm not lost."

She twisted around to stare at me. "You know where we are?"

"Pretty much."

Her voice went up a couple notches. "And you can find that doctor's office?"

"Now that you doubled back some, we're about five blocks northeast of it."

She shrieked, "And you didn't tell me?"

"You're the leader. I'm the follower, remember?"

Oh boy, did she blister me then! She was so loud that somewhere a moose raised its head and looked around. Suddenly she stopped and said, "I don't believe you!"

"Sor—" I clamped my hand over my mouth and rolled my eyes toward her.

Apparently she was giving up trying to turn me from a dork into a—into what? Who knows? Anyway, she didn't yell at me anymore. She just sighed.

I stood up. "Let's go. It's almost six."

"How do you know that?"

"I not only move all the time, I get hungry a lot. I'm six-o'clock hungry."

"You really think you can get us back?"

As we started walking, the leader sort of became the follower. At least she didn't march straight ahead anymore.

"Yeah, I think so. The streets are mostly on a grid, except for that S curve near the park here. You went north instead of south awhile, saw your mistake, and headed west. Now you were going parallel to the road you wanted to be on. You turned south, but we haven't gone far enough south yet, and we're still too far west."

"I don't know when I'm going east or south or whatever."

"You don't have to in a mall. You have that map that says You Are Here."

She made a really disgusted face. "I still

don't believe you. How can you tell which direction you're going?"

I pointed up. "The sun. It's overcast, but the sun still shows up as the brightest part of the sky. Don't feel bad. You haven't had practice. In the malls you like—the fancy, covered ones—you can't see the sun at all."

I decided not to mention that Mom had her pegged just right—likely to get lost at the drop of a compass needle.

She pondered this awhile. Well, actually, I have no idea what she was pondering. At least she wasn't chewing on me.

"Les? This is a family outing, right? So why did your parents bring those other kids along?"

"We're sort of a club. We're the Sugar Creek Gang because we like the Sugar Creek books. Dad told me once that wholesome friends are very important. And the Gang is all wholesome people, so he includes them a lot." There I went again. I wanted to say something deep and important, and it wasn't coming out right.

Did she understand? I glanced at her and couldn't tell. We walked awhile in silence.

Then I pointed. "Right there is where you asked that lady where the mall is. Recognize it?"

"No. And I don't think you—oh, yeah. But why are we coming from this direction? We should be coming from the other direction."

"Because you overshot it, remember? This way." And I headed for the doctor's office.

"I know which way!" she snarled.

You just can't win.

Catherine was lying on a couch in the waiting room. She sat up when we came in. "Mom is getting some prescriptions at the drugstore."

I flopped down to sitting beside her, more tired than I would let on. "We going back tonight or tomorrow?"

"Tonight. Mom called them. They'll take us back out to our boat."

"How you feeling?"

"Horrible."

"That's how you look."

Mom got back a couple minutes later. We climbed into the van wearily. Everyone was weary—for different reasons, I suspect—but weary. Mom stopped at the Colonel's, and we ate chicken on the road. We got to the marina around 10:30 at night.

There were those two boys, just as cheery as when we saw them last. They said, "Leave the van. We'll park it," and put us in the powerboat.

The trip out went a little slower than before. I'm sure that was because it was night. If they hit a floating log—or some fisherman without his running lights on—you would have heard the crash in Seattle.

Catherine dozed, curled up in Mom's arms. I saw Lisa sneer when she climbed into Mom's lap. Probably she figured Catherine was too old for that kind of baby stuff. But when you're sick, what feels better than anything else in the whole world, right?

I just about fell asleep. But then the overcast we'd been living under since we got here began to break up. It was patchy when we left the dock. By the time we were out in the second of three "lakes" (wide spots in the waterway), the patches had dissolved. Haze remained, making the sky milky. But you could see through it.

What did I see? I saw stars. More stars melted into view here and there. It was full moon tonight or close to it. The totally huge moon coasted above the trees. It made the water shine silver, almost as bright as day except in the shaded spots near shore. I loved it—what I guess you'd call the beauty of the moment.

When they delivered us to the boat, everyone was still up except Mike. He had been too sleepy to hold out. They helloed us enthusiastically. They gave us popcorn and soft drinks. Tiny told me about the loon he heard and the black-crowned night heron he saw.

We went to bed.

Well, I didn't go right away. As Mom and Dad disappeared into their bedroom and the other kids all settled in, I went out onto the back deck.

Gerty got up from her folded blanket and greeted me all over again, as if she hadn't licked me half to death the first time. I sat on the deck and rubbed her behind the ears. She curled up at my feet.

The full moon, the glassy water, the quiet, and the dark felt so good. All of it. Back home,

I would sit by my bedroom dormer window like this and talk to God—and be talked to by God sometimes. I did that now. I prayed for Catherine. What a bummer, to be sick on vacation. I prayed nobody else would get it. A lot of people were crowded into a pretty small space here.

I thanked God for the great time, the safe trip to Hibbing, and all the regular stuff you thank Him for. And then I just sat and listened and felt.

I can't tell you how I knew He was talking to me. There weren't any words or anything like that. But I knew He loved us. And I understood something that surprised me. I *didn't* understand how it could be happening. I wasn't doing anything special. In fact, I was doing a pretty poor job, it seemed. When Lisa badmouthed Him and His Son, I didn't stand up for Him the way I should have.

All the same, He was reaching out to Lisa. That wasn't surprising—He reaches out to everyone. The surprising part was, He was doing it through me.

14

Picture a long, slender fish with huge eyes and a mouth with a grin like the Grinch's. The mouth is armed with wicked teeth. They're more like fangs. Picture one of these beauties big enough to weigh in at ten pounds. That's a walleye.

Now picture me catching one.

Well, I pictured myself catching one. But you would probably snicker and say, "Les, that's awfully hard to imagine. Not with your kind of luck."

And you'd be right. Actually, ten-pound walleyes are very rare. They more commonly run two or three pounds. But even two pounds is still a lot of fish, and I set out to catch one.

In fact, we all went fishing the next evening. We had spent the day just messing around. You can have a whole lot of fun doing nothing you can describe later. Somebody might say, "Didn't you guys get bored with no TV, no e-mail, and no place to go?"

And I would reply, "Not for a minute. I can't say what we did. We did nothing. But it took us the whole day."

The first to catch a fish that evening was Mike. He pulled in a small one only about a foot long, and he was as happy as if it had been

Moby Dick. Mike can get happy over just about anything.

As usual, Lisa was too good to stoop to something as low as catching a slimy, cold-blooded creature. But Dad baited a hook and handed the rod to her. He spent maybe twenty minutes showing her how to cast, how to keep the thing from tangling, how to reel in.

And Lisa was actually a very good learner. She picked up on it fast. Pretty soon, she was a fisherman in spite of herself. Dad praised her enthusiastically.

She cast her line out across the water and began reeling in as instructed. She tugged on it. "It's stuck." The end of the line moved side-ways.

"You have a bite!" Dad cried.

He coached her. She played it. When the end of her line got within twenty feet of shore, Dad waded out with the net and scooped it in.

Lisa had not just caught a walleye. She had caught a colossal walleye. It was nowhere near record, but we measured it later that night, and it was seventeen inches. That's colossal when all you're used to seeing are five-inch-long bluegills.

As the fish came ashore, we jumped up and down and cheered and slapped Lisa on the back.

Dad gave her a quick side-by-side hug. "My star pupil!" he boasted.

"Your dinner tomorrow night!" Mom grinned.

Lisa frowned. "But I don't like fish."

Mom didn't skip a beat. The grin stayed. "OK. Someone else's dinner. It's a fine achievement. I'm very proud of you, Lisa!"

For the next hour, until it got too hard to see well, we fished. I, who dreamed of catching a record walleye, caught nothing. Bits got a small one. So did Hannah. Lisa caught a second small one. Two in one evening!

Tiny didn't catch anything, but that might be because he didn't spend much time with a line in the water. He took a long while sketching Lisa's colossal fish. He even drew a head-on view of it.

Lynn didn't get as much fishing in as she might have, either. In the middle of taking pictures, she had to change film rolls.

(Oh, P.S.—Dad didn't catch anything either.)

That night, I asked Tiny if he'd said thank you. He had. Then I went out on the back deck again to commune with Gerty and God, in that order. I took care of Gerty pretty quickly. If you just keep scratching her awhile, she falls asleep.

God is . . . different. Not that He doesn't want you to talk to Him. He's just . . . well . . . God. You know. He's the Lord of the universe way up there, and I'm Les Walker, a puny little kid way down here. The miracle is that He messes with me at all, but He does.

I was hoping He would show me what exactly I ought to be doing for Lisa, or with Lisa, or maybe even to Lisa. Not a clue. Either I wasn't hearing something, or He figured I was doing all right on my own.

I did watch a storm come in, though. The clear sky of evening had been getting thickly cloudy even before we went inside for the night. Now it was so black that not even the moon could punch through it.

Lightning laced across the horizon to the southwest. Distant thunder became nearby thunder. I began to review what the rules were if you get caught outdoors in a lightning storm. I couldn't remember any of them that pertained to boats. I couldn't remember if you get out of the boat or stay in it.

A jagged, blue white streak of lightning came zippering down. It struck the distant island off our stern. Thunder slammed instantly. I got up and went in to rap on Mom and Dad's door.

Mom mumbled something in a sleepy voice.

"Thunderstorm," I said softly. "Should we be doing anything?"

Moments later, Dad came out in nothing but blue jeans. He closed the bedroom door and led me out onto the back deck again. We closed the sliding glass door behind us, but still we kept our voices low.

"Can't sleep?" he asked.

"Yeah, I'm sleepy. I was just out here a few minutes. It's so neat." Should I tell him about talking to God?

"You're right," he said. "It is. And in answer

to your question, no. We don't have to do any-thing."

With the cloud cover, it was too dark to see, but you could hear the rain coming up the lake, roaring closer, closer. It arrived, pelting and slamming, accompanied by very loud thunder. OK, I admit I was a little scared. We stepped back against the glass under the over-hanging top deck, to avoid getting totally soaked. The temperature dropped from 60 to 40 or whatever. Instantly. At any rate, it got drastically cool.

Mike pushed open the glass door and came out. He didn't say anything. He just got very close to Dad.

The violent part of the storm passed before long. The rain remained, drumming so quietly it didn't really mess up the silence much at all. Eventually, Mike went back inside. So did I. Dad closed the bedroom door behind him. I climbed into our top-deck bedroom and lis-tened to the rain hit the roof for a good twenty seconds before I fell asleep.

15

We set sail the next morning after breakfast. I'm not sure that's how you would say it, "set sail." Anyway, we left our camping spot and cruised to another.

Except for some haze that made the blue a little pale, the sky had cleared. We swept a lot of leaves and sticks off the top deck. Then we settled in for the cruise.

Everyone had on a hat except Lisa and me. As you know, I had forgotten mine. She was working on a tan. Mom didn't say anything to her. It must have been a strain on her, because she'd long preached against suntans. My sisters and I all grew up knowing that a suntan is not a sign of robust health. It could be a sign of skin cancer coming in the future.

Lisa, though, was showing off her two-hundred-dollar swimsuit. It was, she announced, one of those suits that lets you get a tan right through the fabric. She stretched out on the deck on a big beach towel and closed her eyes.

"Stop!" Tiny shrieked.

Startled, Dad cut the throttle back. The engine stalled and quit. "What?"

Lisa bolted upright, looking frightened.

Tiny pointed wildly. "On that little island over there, right by the rocks! Look!"

With the kind of excitement that a game show host usually shows, Tiny whipped his binoculars to his face. "A mother loon on her nest!" He gazed at the island.

Lisa moaned, "Oh, for pity's sake! Tiny, you are a total nerd. Absolutely total!" And she lay down again.

The houseboat bobbed, dead in the water. It drifted closer to the island. Now we could all see, even without glasses. A loon sat still as death among tufts of grass near water's edge. She pressed her chin on the ground so that she was nothing more than a dark blob with some white marks, if you looked carefully enough.

Dad watched a few moments and restarted the motor. "We don't want to get so close that we frighten her off her eggs."

The motor rumbled, at work again, and we were on our way. I went below before my sun-cooked nose started to peel. But I could watch out the wall-to-wall windows as we eased into a broad, sweeping cove. The dense woods came down almost to the water in a big C shape. Except for a narrow, sandy beach right in the middle of the cove—the farthest point back—the shore was all rocks. We moved carefully into the open mouth of that broad C.

And this time, I knew what to do. While Dad nosed the houseboat in against the beach, I climbed out on the narrow strip of side deck and picked up the port hawser. That's a fancy term for the rope you tie it up with. I forget where I learned that.

When Mom opened the gate in the rail at the front and jumped over the side, I tossed the line. Mike jumped off the boat's nose right behind her.

My line fell way short and plopped in the water.

"Oh, honestly, Les!" Right behind me, Lisa let fly with a name for me she hadn't used before. "You're such a *loser*. Here! Give me that!"

She hauled in the sloppy-wet line and threw it out again. This time, the end coil made it all the way to shore. Mom scooped it up and tied us into another one of those iron rings.

On the starboard side, Tiny had thrown to Mike. Mike tied his hawser tightly. We were firmly attached to solid land again.

Mom pulled out the gangplank and dropped its loose end in the sand. We all headed for the gangplank and shore.

"Wait!" Dad yelled.

We all paused.

"According to the map, this is a large island, with several deep coves," he warned. "It's going to be very easy to get lost here, so stay close to the campsite. Hear?"

We all promised. We trooped ashore.

Tiny whipped out his sketchbook and started drawing things. Out loud, Lisa declared him a loser.

Mike found some small skipping stones. He spent the next twenty minutes trying to beat his own personal record of four skips. That made him a loser also, and she told him so.

Lynn took pictures. Bits managed to climb a tall snag—a tree sticking out of the water—and declared that the view from up there was awesome. Both were losers; just ask Lisa.

I helped Dad make dinner. Lisa must have been hungry—she didn't call us losers out loud.

I looked at our one solitary little big-enough-to-eat walleye. "I don't think the loaves and fishes thing is going to work this time."

"It worked once." Dad grinned.

"Yeah, but that was for five thousand people. There's only ten of us. Feeding ten off one walleye probably isn't a big enough miracle for God to bother messing with."

"Actually, Les, I don't think the main point of that miracle was the numbers. I think it was that the people would have gone hungry without it. We have plenty of food. Therefore, no miracle needed."

So we thawed ground beef to make burgers for most of us. I made a coating for the fish out of stale bread crumbs, milk and garlic, paprika and sage. We dipped the fish in that and grilled it last.

This site had a picnic table on shore. We ate there, six at the table and four at a folding table we set up beside it. Everyone had some of the fish, just to say we all tried it.

I didn't mention anything, but I noticed that Lisa took a few bites, also. Maybe she didn't like fish, but curiosity obviously got the better of her.

It was Lynn and Bits's turn to clean up the

kitchen. Tiny went off with his sketchbook, which, I learned, also served as a journal. Dad read on the top deck.

Mom looked around. "I don't see Lisa anywhere."

I was getting used to this keep-tabs-on-Lisa thing, not that I much liked it. All she ever did was yell at me. "Want me to go look?"

"If you would, please."

Hi ho, off we go.

This particular island had no trails leading away from the campsite. Apparently you weren't supposed to go anywhere here. So I just sort of worked my way along the shore, around the point, and into another bay.

From way up ahead, I heard Gerty bark cheerfully. Ah. Where Gerty was, Lisa would be. The dog wouldn't leave camp except with her. I almost turned around and went back. Mom didn't say I had to talk to her. She just wanted me to see where she was.

But I kept going anyway. Sure enough, up ahead in a shallow cove stood Gerty, knee-deep in water. She was facing my way, listening to me approach. She barked.

So I barked back.

Lisa's voice called, "Who's there?"

"Only us dogs," I replied.

I heard outraged mutterings.

She was sitting on a huge flat rock by water's edge. Smoke curled up from her hand. I kind of figured it wasn't her fingers on fire.

She'd been caught red-handed, of course.

She didn't try to hide her cigarette or anything. She just watched, her nose in the air, as I climbed across the rocks to her.

I fought off Gerty's enthusiastic greeting the best I could and settled on Lisa's rock beside her. That journal Mom had given her lay on the rock behind her. One of the pens was stuck in it, holding a place. I didn't say anything about it.

I figured I really ought to say something about smoking, though. On the other hand, she wouldn't listen to anything a certified dork had to say, anyway.

So all I said was, "They say that stuff can kill you, you know."

"So what?"

"Living's no fun if you're dead."

"It's no fun if you're alive, either."

I thought about that a moment. "Y'know, you are so totally wrong, I don't know where to start with an answer. So I guess I won't."

She let the silence ride for a while. Then she said, "I'm still mad at you for not loaning me that money. You still have all the allowance they gave you."

"Not all of it. We bought postcards. They sold them on that ore freighter. It worked out real well, actually. We brought stamps and address labels from home. Bits has this computer program that makes mailing labels. All of us Creekers put our addresses into her machine, and she ran the labels. So in Duluth, all we had to do was sit down while we were eat-ing lunch, stick the labels on, write hello on the cards, and mail them. Now the postcards will get back before we do."

Her voice dripped acid. "You loonies think you are so smart, don't you?"

She opened herself up on that one. I couldn't resist. "We're smart enough to not smoke."

"And you can't wait to run back and tell your daddy."

"Nah. He already knows. And Mom. You can't slip diddly past those two. Believe me. I've spent a lifetime trying."

Silence again.

It was almost dark. I wanted to get back. But I kind of hated to leave her. I was afraid she'd walk away in the wrong direction again.

She stubbed out her cigarette and stood up. "So who sent you to check up on me?" She picked up her journal.

"Mom. You have a history of getting lost."

"Har, har, har." But she waited for me to take the lead going back, I noticed.

We started working our way along the shoreline. It was so dark now, it wasn't easy. Gerty bounced around ahead of us. It wasn't hard, apparently, if you're a dog.

Suddenly she said, "I searched your parents' bedroom. Did you know that?"

I about fell off the rock I was climbing across. I turned to look at her. "Why in the world would you do that?"

"Trying to find their stash. There's gotta be a stash aboard that scow somewhere."

"A stash of *what?*" I continued on, trying to see rocks in near total darkness.

"I cannot believe you are that stupid, Les! You're putting on an act, right?"

"You're lying, right? I cannot believe you'd search my parents' stuff."

"Pot. Crack. Beer. Whatever. I'm still sure they have booze stuffed somewhere. I just can't find it."

"Well, knock yourself out if you want. You're not going to find anything. You know, Lisa, up until this trip I thought my sisters were the two biggest weirdos in the whole world. Always telling me what to do. Bossing me around. But I'm never going to bad-mouth them again. Not after meeting you."

It took us twenty minutes to go that quarter mile or so. Gerty bounced into camp a hundred feet ahead of us.

Dad was sitting on the deck, watching for us. He stood up when we got there. All he said was, "Don't cut it so close next time, please."

That "please" didn't fool me one second. And now I didn't know what to do. Mom thought I ought to keep an eye on Lisa. But Dad had just let me know, if I stayed out till dark again on this trip, I was in trouble.

16

It rained most of the next day. Not to worry. We sat around playing chess and checkers and Monopoly and had a high old time. In fact, Lynn had brought her new Monopoly game, the national parks version. Yellowstone instead of Boardwalk, trails instead of railroads, Hot Springs and Edison instead of utilities—but the Chance, Community Chest, and Jail spaces were still there. It was the same game as always, only different. We had a ball!

Lynn took a few minutes to take photos, as always. I don't know what Tiny wrote in his journal, but at least he didn't draw pictures.

Lisa was too sophisticated to play games, of course. (I can't say she was too grown-up, understand, because our token grown-ups, Mom and Dad, played Skip-Bo most of the afternoon.) So she was the banker. She was a good banker, too, quick with the calculations and able to make instant change. And believe me, she did love to foreclose on our properties whenever she got the chance. I think she had more fun than the players did.

The grill stayed dry under the top-deck overhang, so we kids decided to grill something for supper. Surprise! Dad whipped a plain brown wrapper out of the freezer: five

T-bone steaks. He opined that if we had to grill something, we might as well go for the gold, sort of.

You cannot believe how much thought went into that meal. It wasn't the potatoes (Lynn and Bits) or the salad (Tiny and Hannah) or setting the table (Dad). It was figuring out how each person preferred his or her steak, and then matching them up correctly. If we were grilling five steaks for ten people, that was two people to a steak. You can't do half a steak rare and the other half well-done. See the problem?

Anyway, we finally figured all that out. We ended up dividing one steak in half because the numbers didn't come out even. Since I was a future great chef, I took charge of the actual cooking.

Know what? The meal turned out just fine. Everyone got his steak done the way he liked it. Mostly. Well, in some cases. And everything ended up done at the same time. In other words, one thing didn't get cold while we waited for another to finish cooking.

Dad cleaned up and stowed away the cooking stuff. The rest of us scattered.

It had quit raining, but the island and the boat were soggy wet. Mike decided that, during rain, the fish hid under the boat to keep dry. So he got out a rod and tried fishing down under the hull. I don't know if he was serious or not. I hope not.

Bits decided to fish off the stern, like sensible folks.

Lisa dug out her movie magazines.

Tiny and Lynn got a deep-thinker chess game going.

Catherine and Hannah read.

Gerty fell asleep in the middle of the traffic lane. We all had to step over her every time we went anywhere. Typical dog.

And even though it was wet as a gator's tail, I decided to take a walk. For one thing, it was a good way to pray. Sitting out on deck wasn't going to work well with everyone doing his own thing all over the boat. For another, it was a great night for a walk.

Everything dripped, so I wore an old T-shirt and cutoffs. I knew I'd have to change when I got back. I walked out and around the point opposite the direction Lisa had taken.

The overcast ended an inch above the horizon. Soon the sun got low enough to sneak out from under the clouds. Instantly, the water danced gold. The evergreens turned gold, especially the tips of the branches with their new growth. Gold washed the shrubs and rocks.

I picked myself a nice, smooth boulder that sat in the lake where the water met the rocks and climbed out to it. Together with another rock on it, it made a perfect chair. I sat on the flat rock and leaned back on the rock behind me. I stretched my legs out and enjoyed the gold. Who says rocks can't be comfortable?

Not totally comfortable. I'd gotten dripped on enough that my T-shirt was wet. So were my shoes and socks. And my legs were wet. So I got pretty cold pretty quickly. No matter. The view was worth it.

And then there was the silence. This was genuine silence, not the fake silence you get in town. In town there's always a motor somewhere. Sometimes it's the heating or air conditioning system in your own house, or the refrigerator purring. Sometimes a siren howls somewhere off in the distance. Planes fly over, and cars rush by. Trains toot at crossings. Dogs bark.

Here? Nothing. That's what I mean by genuine silence.

Somewhere out on the water, a loon called. It was funny thing: that didn't so much break the silence as emphasize it.

For starters I thanked God for helping Catherine get better. She actually seemed human again. And I thanked Him, too, for sparing the rest of us from whatever she got sick from. That was an answer to prayer right there.

Then I simply sat back and listened to nothing.

"Aha!" Lisa's shrill voice behind me made me jump two feet.

I twisted around to look at her. "Aha what?"

"Put both hands up."

I did. "Let me guess. This is a stickup."

She came climbing out to me. She looked at me. And looked. And her face fell.

"Can I put my arms down now?" I moved over to make room for her in my chair. "And why are you so disappointed?"

"I was sure you were smoking. Why else would you sneak way out here?"

"Item one, I didn't sneak. If I really wanted to sneak, you wouldn't have seen me leave. Item two, you don't want to know what I'm doing."

"Yes, I do."

"Praying."

"No, I don't." She stared at me, just plain disgusted looking. "Yeah, sure. Praying."

"Well, to be honest, not praying exactly. I did that when I got here. Now it's more like, God and I talk."

"Uh-huh." She pulled her cigarette pack out of her windbreaker pocket and tipped it toward me.

"No, thanks."

She shrugged, got one out, and lit up.

And here I have to admit that there was something about what she just did that looked very—I don't know the word to use. Appealing? Tempting? She looked . . . cool. She looked like what little kids wished they looked like.

I could see why kids might get hooked on tobacco accidentally. It looked good, in a twisted sort of way. You try it out because you think you look good doing it. Except that you don't look good, not really. You look stupid, when you think about it. Let's set fire to some leaves and let the smoke swirl around in our lungs awhile. Who knows? It might cause a disease, but so what? We look cool.

Right.

She looked at me as if I were the world's weirdest weirdo. "You really came here to pray? Really?"

"Really."

"And you're not ashamed?"

"Of what?"

"It's so nerdy! So dorky!"

And a thought came to mind so suddenly that I wondered if maybe the Lord had put it there to help me out. Otherwise, I wouldn't have had an answer.

"Dorky according to who? Why do you think you're a hundred percent right about who's a loser and who's dorky? Maybe you're wrong, and I'm right. I mean, hey, I'm talking to God. You can't get to anybody higher than that."

"You just think you are."

And I put it in the simplest terms possible. "I know Him."

She glared at me. "I can tell I'm not going to win this argument. Not when you're so pig-headed." And she turned her attention to the lake and the view.

When it came to sunsets, she had the attention span of a butterfly in a clover patch. She sat there for only a couple of seconds before she started fidgeting. "Aren't you afraid your parents will catch us and they'll punish you for smoking, too?"

"Nah. They know I don't. But they'll come down hard on you."

"Who cares? They're not my parents."

I remembered she had mentioned that her dad took her first stash of cigarettes away from her. "So do you smoke in front of your parents?"

She had her mouth open to answer before she realized what she would be saying. "You're pretty sneaky for a little kid, you know that?"

I stood up. "Enjoy your weeds. I'm going to head back. It'll be dark soon."

She stubbed out her cigarette, and it was still long. "Wait up. I'll go, too."

And so Miss I-Don't-Know-Which-Way-Is-Up and I headed back.

I guess we got back in time, because Dad wasn't sitting on the deck tapping his foot impatiently.

And Mike had caught a sucker under the boat.

17

By now you may have grasped that Lisa was a royal pain. Back a million years or so, when we sat on a picnic bench in Sugar Creek Park, Bits had warned us that Lisa would spoil all our fun. Her warning didn't come true exactly, but she had Lisa pegged right on. Trouble.

Lisa spoiled some of mine. I wanted to hang out, and instead I followed her around to make sure she didn't get lost. You didn't have to worry about losing anyone else. Even Catherine had better woods sense than Miss Sophisticate, and Catherine can't find her way around a one-room house.

The next day was cloudy but warm. Mom said, "Let's go to Canada."

Canada?

It turned out that Canada was only about a mile away, on the other side of the lake. Voyageurs is right on the border. I mean right on it.

So away we went. We set up the folding picnic table and put out a cooler and stuff to make our campsite look lived in while we were gone. We didn't want someone taking our site while we were cavorting in a foreign country.

As we approached the other shore, I noted that Canada looked exactly like the United

States. It was all flatland, forest, and lakeshore, the same as everywhere else up here.

We chugged up to a little pier and tied our boat at the dock. There we were greeted by some customs officers. They asked, so we told them we were United States citizens. They asked where we were from and how long we were staying.

Mom replied, "Indiana," and, "Just long enough to get ice cream."

The two men nodded, smiling. "Enjoy your stay."

Ice cream? The day was looking better all the time.

Was there shopping in Canada? You bet! I am not normally a shopper. I hate going to the mall with Mom and my sisters; I always end up carrying stuff. But this was different. This was Canada.

The ten of us trooped up a steeply sloping, peaceful, tree-shaded path toward the store.

"So this is Canada!" Lynn yanked out her ever present camera and started snapping. There was a lot to snap. I didn't see any houses, but obviously people lived here. And they planted lots of flowers in the summer. Maybe it was to make up for the long, long winters. We followed Mom and Dad up the slope to the store.

Now when you think of a store, you're likely to think of Wal-Mart or Home Depot or at least something with eight or ten aisles. For starters, this store was little more than a wooden cabin painted white. The door was like the front door of any house. I assumed there were rooms in back where the owner lived, but the store part consisted of two tiny rooms that were living-room size. Only one of them was big enough for two narrow aisles. Along part of one wall, they sold soft drinks and ice cream. Mom announced we'd buy that last.

The rest of this tiny shop sold Canadian souvenirs—everything from mittens to T-shirts had north country themes. Moose figured prominently. So did wolves and trout.

I wandered around the place, admiring stuff. I didn't see much to buy. What would I do with fridge magnets? Or a windsock?

Mom started stacking her collection of purchases on the counter. Dad frowned and looked at her. "Christmas presents," was all she said.

What a great idea! Bits and I looked at each other and nodded. So in the middle of summer in a foreign country, I did some Christmas shopping.

I can't explain it exactly. But I can tell you, there is a lot of delight in doing something goofy like that.

As I paid for my choices, I realized that one of us was not going to buy anything. Not trinkets, not souvenirs, not gifts. Not ice cream.

Now what? I knew what Mom and Dad thought about kids living within their means. When they said, "You learn when you're young, and you won't have to worry about failure when you're grown-up," I believed them. Still, this was pretty hard. I mean, here's this special occasion on a special vacation and . . .

So I found Tiny and mumbled in his ear. And Bits. And Lynn and Mike. And Hannah and Catherine, too.

Then I found Lisa. It wasn't easy. I had to leave the store. Part of the way down that shady path, off to the side, was an arbor-covered bench. She sat there moping. As much as she tried to look uninterested and bored, you could see she was moping.

I sat down beside her. She glared at me and refused to move over. I felt unwelcome. And I realized that she was likely to refuse my offer unless I worded it very, very carefully.

"Lisa, do you know what a trip allowance is?"

"Money on a trip."

"Right. It's separate from your regular allowance." I asked God to help me here. I couldn't do this alone. "This is our last stop. Last chance to spend money on the trip." I handed her some bills. "Since you're short, and we had this left over, we figured you could use it, since we can't anymore."

She stared a hole through me. "I'm not a charity case!"

"Oh, come on, Lisa! So far you haven't done a thing but sneer at us and bad-mouth us and call us losers. You try every which way to get out of doing any work. You don't carry your share, and you're a lousy friend. Why would you ever think we would spend charity on you? This is leftover money. And we owe you nothing. Exactly all of nothing. Understand?"

I stuffed the cash in her hand. Then I got

up quickly and walked back up the slope into the store.

Would it work? I didn't know. I kept praying.

When I got back, the rest of the gang had bought their stuff. Now, each in turn was ordering an ice cream cone. I fell in at the back of the line.

Bits, the next to the last, turned to me. "So? How'd the little snip take it?"

"We'll see. She wasn't real receptive."

She wagged her head. "I still don't know why you thought of it, but it feels right. I don't know why. Know what I mean?"

"Yeah." But not because Bits was real cloquent about explaining it.

The line moved as slowly as a millipede with ankle weights. Finally it was my turn to order. I got a double dip of chocolate. There is no substitute for real chocolate ice cream.

I could see outside through the glass front door. Lynn had grabbed one of the customs persons and handed him her camera. She was lining everyone up by the door for a group shot. Peachy. Another group shot.

I licked a drip. Delicious! I headed for the door. And what a surprise I got!

I had to step aside because Lisa was coming in. "Don't leave without me," she said. "I'm going to get some ice cream."

The surprise was her eyes. They were red and puffy.

That's right. She'd been crying.

18

Hey, Tiny!" I yelled. "Did you thank God today?"

"Sure did," he yelled back.

We gave each other the high sign and went about our business.

Out by the boat stern, Tiny stood in water almost waist deep, pursuing his business of fishing. Yesterday he had landed a walleye. Now he was all caught up in the thrill of the chase. Tonight he wanted to catch a bigger one.

I stood on the front deck at a little folding table beside the gas grill. I was pursuing my business of creating a delectable dish for ten using nothing but canned stuff. With only a couple days left of our week, we were about out of fresh and frozen. It was down to canned.

Last night I had created a masterpiece, salmon Mornay Florentine. My own recipe. We had cheese to use up, powdered milk, canned spinach, and two cans of pink salmon. I don't know who in the world thought canned spinach would be a good thing to bring on vacation. But since we had it, I used it as a dark green bed to serve the salmon on. A thin layer of spinach, a glob of salmon, the cheese sauce, artfully drizzled over the top. There! *Voila!*—as the French say.

It looked great. It tasted OK. Lisa refused to touch it. Six of the remaining nine picked at it and smiled bravely. Mike, Mom, and I devoured it. Three in ten is not a good response to a new recipe. Especially when one of the only three who like it is its creator.

Lisa parked in the sliding glass doorway, her arms folded, that familiar scowl on her face. "You did that just to bug me, didn't you?"

"Did what?"

"Yelled at Tiny about thanking God."

"That bugs you?"

"I'm getting really sick of getting God rubbed in my face all the time. God this. Jesus that. It's getting more than a little old. And you can tell your father I said that, too."

"Why? He knows. He knows everything you think and feel. Your deepest thoughts, the stuff you keep hidden." And then I let my mean streak show. "Oh, wait!" I corrected myself. "You don't mean the Father God. You mean Dad. Why don't you tell him yourself?"

She called me a name and went back inside.

Bits had to step aside quickly to avoid being run over. My fellow Sugar Creeker came outside beside me. "So what's the menu tonight? Not more spinach, I hope."

"Nope. We used it up."

Bits glanced in at Lisa and jacked her voice up twenty decibels. "No more spinach?" She yelled, "We're thankful!"

From inside, a door slammed. It would

have to be the bathroom door. That's the only one that Lisa could have swung shut so hard.

"That wasn't nice, Bits." I grinned.

"Daddy's little girl loves being naughty. So what are you making if it's not spinach?"

"Chicken pot pie. We have lots of dry egg noodles, two canned chickens, a couple cans of potatoes and onions left, and canned carrots. I'll mix it all together and make a biscuit dough topping. We can bake it in the gas grill. With the top clamped down tight, the grill is an oven. Really neat."

"I suppose now you want a grill like this for your birthday."

I shook my head. "Roller blades first. Then a gas grill."

For a moment, she watched me stir my mixture. "You know, Les, maybe you *will* become a great chef someday." She started to leave, paused, and turned. "But not because of that salmon and spinach!" and she jogged on down the gangplank to shore.

Some people just don't know what's good.

That night, the chicken pot pie *was* good. Maybe even great. At least nobody picked at it. They all dug right in and cleaned it up. No leftovers.

And Tiny didn't catch anything, so there was no fish, either.

Afterward, Bits and Lynn cleaned up the kitchen. I got my fighter plane model out and worked at it on the table awhile, but not for long.

I wandered outside and down the ramp.

Mike and Dad were conducting a two-contestant fishing derby. You should have heard those two blowhards brag as each tried to get a bite before the other did.

Tiny was out on the point with his binoculars. I have no idea what he was looking at.

Mom, Catherine, and Hannah were playing Parchesi.

Lisa, I assumed, was off having a smoke—although Gerty was still here, curled up out on the back deck.

No one told me to go find Lisa, exactly, but that seemed to be the job I'd fallen into. Everyone else was doing something. So I walked down the lakeshore looking for her.

I saw the world's biggest turtle lying on a rock. It slid into the water as I approached. The turtle's dive was a cannonball Mike sure would have envied. Of course, if you're going to cannonball, having a fifteen-inch-wide flat shell doesn't hurt.

Away out across the water, the loon yodeled. I assumed only one pair of loons per lake. Tiny also thought that was right. For every lake its loon. How great!

No Lisa. She hadn't gone out this way, so, obviously, she went the other way. I returned to the houseboat.

Mike was putting away his fishing rod. He grinned. "Your dad finally caught something!"

"Did you, too?"

Still grinning, he paused for effect. "Yeah!

A sucker. He bet me I couldn't catch anything before he got a walleye, and I did."

Bits, Lynn, and Tiny joined us.

"Seen Lisa?" I asked.

"Not since dinner." Bits scowled. "Is Miss Perfect lost again?"

"Doubt it." I dipped my head toward where I'd just been. "But she's not along the shore out that way."

Tiny shrugged. "I'll go along with you to find her."

"Me, too. I got nothing else to do now." Bits nodded.

Lynn came, too, as it turned out. She just didn't say so. And Mike went *sprong, sprong* out ahead of us, the way he usually does.

So there went the five of us, sort of pouring across the rocks. We jumped and laughed, making jokes.

That was one of the very best things about the Sugar Creek Gang. We fit together so well. I am really down on girls in general and some girls in particular. I used to think it was because I had two older sisters. But some boys I grew up with in Seattle had all brothers. They weren't any happier about the female half of the world than I was—except mothers, of course. They're not really females. So I really surprised myself when I found myself liking Lynn and Bits just as much as the guys.

Oh, sure, we'd get mad at each other sometimes. But then you say to yourself, *That's how this person is. Live with it.* And we'd live with it.

It was a gift from God that Bits and Lynn were just the same as Tiny and Mike and me. Nobody got mad or huffy if they got teased. Boy or girl. If it really bothered them, they said so, and the rest would quit. Once in a while we all found ourselves just sitting around because we couldn't think of anything to do. When we'd get bored, we'd get cranky, but even then, we got along.

This time, we all had a mission, however temporary: go rescue Lisa, whether she wanted rescuing or not. No boredom now! When we left the houseboat behind, we forgot to notice the weather.

We really, really should not have forgotten that.

19

How far did we go when we set out to find Lisa? We didn't know. For one thing, the way we were laughing and goofing off, we didn't keep track of the time. For another, the island's edge looped in and bulged out. Sometimes it pushed out to make a point, a headland. At other times it dipped in, creating a shallow bay.

And then we came to one of those bays that carved itself into the island's shore. The whole area was really low and boggy. There was no way to get around the bay by following the shoreline, because the shoreline was all muskeg—marshy stuff. Tufts of short grass sat in water. You could not even hop from tuft to tuft without getting wet.

Bits said out loud what we all were thinking. "We might as well turn around."

Lynn nodded. "She's not going to try to cross that. She would turn back or try to go around it."

"Do you think we ought to try going around it a little way?" asked Tiny.

"Nah," Mike said. "Nobody normal going to wade around all that. Let's go home."

"But . . ." I was thinking. "This is Lisa we're talking about, folks. She's not normal. Do you think she might see this and say to herself:

Those dummies will never expect me to go around it? And so she goes around it just to make us wrong."

"Yep," said Bits. "That's Lisa, all right."

So we headed inland to work a path around the low, boggy patch.

What a grunt! Instead of going uphill as we turned away from the lake, we must have gone downhill slightly. We'd expected the boggy patch to get narrower. Then we'd get around it and go back to the lakeshore. Instead, the marshy land got wider and wider. It just kept driving us farther away from the shore. Not only that, it got wetter and wetter.

From the knees down, we were all splashed and soaked in a few minutes. The trees here were small and all crowded together. It was hard to get through the woods. And the bushes growing underneath made it all the harder. Impossible, sometimes. A lot of old dead trees lay every which way, like jackstraws, among the live ones. Their spongy trunks were so wet that seedling trees were growing up out of them. You would expect toadstools, moss, and lichens to be growing in the decayed bark of a long-dead tree. But whole trees?

Mike was the first to give it up, probably because he had the shortest legs. Therefore he had to work the hardest. He sat down on a fallen log. "You guys can keep going, but this is too much for me. I'm going back."

Actually, resting was not a bad idea. I sat down beside him. "I say we don't split up.

That's a sure way for someone to get really lost."

Actually, resting was a bad idea. The wet from the tree soaked into my jeans instantly. Now my bottom was wet as well as my feet. And cold. Very cold.

Bits sat down beside me. I poked her. "Up!"

She stood up again instantly. "Huh?"

"It's wet."

"I don't care." She plopped down beside me again. "I gotta rest. This is terrible."

That smart cookie Lynn leaned back against a living, standing-up tree. She seemed to be staying dry. "I can guarantee that Lisa did not go this far. Not in this marsh. She's not strong enough, and she's not motivated enough."

Tiny nodded. He must not have worried too much about wet jeans either, because he sat down on a smaller log nearby. "I been noticing something else. We're not in thick woods anymore."

I looked around. He was right.

"All these trees that fell over, nothing big has grown in to replace them. There's lots of open patches."

"But the sky is so dark we didn't notice. Look!" Bits was pointing up at black and lowering clouds.

Mike was staring at the sky, too. "I think more than just our jeans are gonna be wet soon! That sure looks like rain to me."

Tiny pulled his sketchbook out of his shirt and his colored pencils out of his back pocket.

He opened to the next blank page and said, "Gather 'round. This is what I think."

Lynn lurched herself erect and came over to watch beside Tiny's elbow.

Tiny drew an X. "This is the houseboat. OK? And here's that cove it's moored in. Now. We went off around this way, OK?" He drew a line sort of like the lakeshore, with dips and bulges.

"North is up, right?" Lynn asked.

"North is up. This way. That means we've been going more or less south, minus the ins and outs. Probably angling west a little." He drew a scribble. "This is the marsh. And when we tried to go around it, we went like this . . ." And he drew still another line.

I studied his sketch a moment. "Then if that's accurate, or even kind of accurate—or even not very accurate—if we go south, we'll get back to the shore quicker."

"Lots quicker!" Mike was getting back some of his enthusiasm. "Because when we were coming along the shore, wasn't no marshy land beside us. So you get out of this stuff by going south."

Bits snorted. "Great. So who's got a compass?"

I knew the answer to that.

Nobody.

So we didn't know which way was south.

"Which way did we come from?" I asked. "Exactly, I mean."

"That way." Mike pointed. "I was coming

right toward this log. I was so tired, I turned around and sat down on it, 'stead of climbing over it. So we go that way to go back the way we came."

I raised my hands in a "see?" gesture. "So that's west. Simple."

"Maybe not." Tiny looked grim. "I read someplace that when you're in tight woods like this, and you can't see the sun, you start walking in circles. You don't mean to. It just happens. We might have gotten into walking in circles back there."

"So what you're saying is"—Bits looked just as grim—"we don't know which way anything is."

We were lost.

20

Well, doesn't that throw a kink in your garden hose!

Here we were, the whole gang of us, lost somewhere on a very large island. Totally lost. And we didn't really know which way was up, let alone which way was north.

"Your dad will wait up for us," Bits assured us.

I did not feel the least bit assured. "But he's going to give us plenty of time to come back. It's going to be dark before he decides he ought to start looking for us. Remember the last time I was late getting back? It was dark."

"And when he gets to that boggy cove," Tiny added, "will he know enough to come inland?"

Lynn didn't look assured either. "And if he does come inland, will he go exactly the same way we did? If his route is just slightly different from ours, we'll all miss each other. Even in these fairly open woods, you can't see very far."

"You can't see at all in the dark." Mike looked gloomy. "Now what?"

"Pray." Tiny said it so casually.

I thought about Lisa and how she complained that we talked about God too much. Instead of trying to be being cute and smart-alecky, I should have just told her the truth. That the Lord is not something we merely talk about. He's real. He's with us. I felt guilty. And sad too. What a great opportunity to tell her about Jesus, and I blew it.

We prayed the way Dad's men's group at church sometimes prayed. Tiny started it off by thanking God for taking care of us so far. Mike added something about making the weather hold off. Lynn added a bit, and Tiny thought of something else. So did I. For about ten minutes, each of us talked to God separately, and yet we were together.

Finally, no one spoke for a few moments, so Tiny closed the praying with "In Jesus' name."

Mike was bobbing up and down again, sort of. He's the only person I ever knew who could be moving when he wasn't moving. "We better get started. Which way?"

"I been thinking about that." Tiny stood up. "Mike says we came from that direction. We were sort of strung out in a line, right? Following each other."

We nodded.

"So," he went on, "we probably kept going in pretty much a straight line. That article I read—the one saying you can go in circles—it said to keep that from happening you drag a long pole, a limb or something, behind you. That helps keep you going straight. Five of us all strung out were more or less a straight pole. Know what I mean?"

Lynn bobbed her head. "We probably

wouldn't all bend in one direction or another at once."

"Right. So if that way is probably west, this is probably south."

"Wait." Bits shook her head. "This island is so big, if we go east or north even accidentally, it's going to take us farther in. We'll get more lost."

"We gotta take that chance," Tiny said. "We're likely going to end up spending the night in the woods. We can't do it here in this marsh. We can't sit or lie down without getting wet. And we can't afford to get really chilled. Hypothermia. We need solid land."

"We need a long pole. Keep from going in circles, like Tiny says." I started looking around.

We found a long branch that would do until we came upon a better one. It came off a fir tree or some other evergreen and was fairly fresh. With my pocketknife, I cut the little branches and twigs off it and handed it to Tiny. He must have seen a picture or description to show how to use it.

"Let's go." Mike led off.

Tiny started forward behind Mike. He laid the narrow end of the pole on his right shoulder and gripped it with his right hand. It dragged along behind him.

We struggled and helped each other and struggled some more. Once in a while I'd look up at a patch of sky. The heavy clouds made it dark, but so did lack of sun. It was going to be really dark before long.

"Stop." Bits was breathing heavily. "Since

we can't see far ahead, let's start yelling. Maybe we're not as far from someone as we think. All together." She began it, and we all joined in.

"Hey!"

Before we did that, the woods were silent. That shout made the woods more silent still.

We listened carefully. Nothing. Mike continued on.

A few minutes later, we stopped and shouted again.

Silence.

Then Mike raised a hand. "Listen!"

I didn't hear anything.

Again, five voices at once rang out. *"Hey!"*

The tiniest, most distant, barely audible voice came from somewhere.

We cheered. *"Hey!"* Louder still. Yes, Lord!

Again, a response.

"Which way was it?" Tiny looked all around. "I couldn't tell."

"I think that way," said Lynn, pointing.

And Mike was pointing in about the same direction.

So we went that way. When we yelled, *"Hey!"* again, the voice sounded a little closer.

Lynn was panting now. "That's a woman's voice. Not your Dad's, Les."

"That means he's probably out looking for us and Mom is waiting at the houseboat. So we're headed back to the boat!" I love it when I can think something out like that. I read a lot of mysteries, and the hero always figures out the bad guy with logic like that.

We were definitely headed toward the voice, and the voice didn't seem to be moving. That added more evidence to my guess that we were headed for the houseboat.

We left the bog behind, finally, and started walking on solid ground. Although our feet were soaking wet, at least we weren't slopping in mud and wetness anymore.

One minor problem was that once we got out of the marshy area, the woods closed down around us. No more open places. No more sunlight, not even the little bit we'd been getting.

Tiny found himself a better pole—longer and cleaner. He dumped the first and took up the second.

Mike stopped, and we yelled again. He frowned. "That's not your mama, Les. That's just a girl."

"Then they left Catherine and Hannah at the boat, and they're both out looking!"

"So we all get back all right, but they get lost!" Bits plowed onward, her head down.

"No," Lynn replied. "Surely at least one of them, and probably both of them, heard us yelling. So they'll be starting back to the houseboat by now, too."

"And remember, Mom and Dad can talk to each other," I added. "They both have cell phones." Soon we would all be together. I couldn't wait!

I could not believe how tangled and close this woods had become. If Tiny didn't have that pole we could easily have gone in circles forever.

Finally, the woods opened up a little. The evergreen needles made a firm duff under our feet that didn't give with every step. It wasn't exactly easier going, because we still had lots of downed wood and branches to climb through, and plenty of brush, but it seemed easier.

And then, we came to a boulder, right there in the middle of the flat woods.

And on that boulder sat Lisa.

"It's about time," she whined. "What took you so long?"

21

"What do you mean, you don't know where we are?" Lisa looked ready to rip us all in two. "What did you come out here to get me for, if you don't know where we are?"

She looked about as miserable as a body can look. She had scratched her cheek so deeply that it oozed a bit of blood. Her cute shorts and halter top did not protect her from the brush. Scratches etched across her legs and arms told the world that. And the mud! She had fallen to her knees in mud at least once. I noticed she'd sat in it, too.

And she had been crying again. Her eyes were all puffy and her face streaked. She had not brought tissues for her runny nose, and a halter top doesn't give you any sleeve to wipe your nose with.

I was so disappointed I felt like crying, too. I had myself all convinced that we had nearly reached the houseboat. Now we still had no idea where the houseboat was—or even the lakeshore, for that matter.

Tiny looked grim again. "No time to stand around moping. We need shelter and a fire. It has to be a pretty big shelter too, to hold all six of us. We'll use the pole here and these two trees to start building it from. Anybody got any fishing line with them?"

Nobody did.

"Then we'll just have to wedge stuff together."

All of us but Lynn and Lisa had pocket-knives. That's all you really absolutely have to have—a pocketknife.

"Les, let's you and I gather evergreen branches, lots of them."

Mike scowled. "They won't burn!"

"For the roof. They'll be rainproof. Lynn and Bits and Lisa, you guys gather firewood."

Lynn picked up a stick. "This stuff is awfully wet, Tiny."

"High wood is dry wood. Try breaking dead stuff off the trees."

There's another reason the Sugar Creek Gang was the best bunch in the world—we worked together perfectly. With Tiny directing us as he worked, we all got busy.

Bits and Lynn started to pull the dead lower branches off the standing trees. Lisa didn't know what to do. When she slid down off her rock and tried to walk, she limped.

"I turned my ankle," she complained. "It hurts!"

Bits glared at her. "This is no time to fake anything to get out of work, Lisa. We need you! It's going to get cold, and none of us has a jacket."

"I'm not faking it! I had to quit walking, it hurt so much."

Lynn handed her a branch. "We'll gather

them. You break them up and stack them. You can do that standing in one spot."

I was kind of surprised that Lisa dug in as well as she did and started doing what she was told. I expected more complaining but nothing constructive.

We strung up poles to make a lean-to—you know, a roof with one side on the ground and the other side raised. I could see that fishing line would have been really handy to tie the poles to each other and to tree trunks. Tiny took off his T-shirt and cut it into thin strips. The "string" he made that way had a lot of give to it, but if you wrapped it tight enough, it worked OK.

The longest, heaviest pole we could find went from tree to tree, head high. We tied the narrow ends of three shorter poles to the one at the top, and their other ends lay on the ground at an angle. They were a little crooked, so the roof quickly developed a weird wave to it.

We tied sticks crosswise between the three angled limbs. The final layer was not poles or sticks but greenery.

We cut many green branches and laid them across the bottom sticks, so that their tips rested on the ground. Then we laid a second row. The cut ends were uphill, so that the rain would run off.

Lisa looked at the huge pile of wood beside her. "This is more than enough!"

"It isn't half enough. We're going burn a

lot of wood tonight." Tiny, the tallest, reached some dead branches that the girls could not and snapped them off. "Here."

When Lynn climbed up on Bits's shoulders, those two really started dragging the wood down! Mike quit cutting roof branches and started helping with firewood.

Ten minutes later, it started to rain. But branches on the forest trees kept the rain from reaching the ground right away. We heard it up there, and we got an occasional drop, but we were able to keep building. Lisa quit doing firewood in favor of helping us thatch the roof. She had long arms, and she could reach as high as Tiny. Lynn and Bits stuffed our firewood in under the roof to keep it dry.

We worked until the rain reached us through the forest canopy. By then the lean-to was big enough to hold us, and we crawled inside. Tiny brushed together duff from the forest floor for tinder.

Lisa sniffed. "I suppose you're going to rub two Boy Scouts together to start a fire."

"No, you're going to start it with your lighter," he said.

Of course! I had forgotten that Lisa had a lighter. And apparently so had she.

Even with a lighter, it took a while to get a fire going at the opening of the lean-to. Tiny fed it little things and then larger things.

The rain started pelting down in earnest. We had a couple of drippy little leaks in our green hotel, but nothing serious. After sulking awhile, the fire suddenly got going. It roared up, warm and bright and very friendly.

I took off my shoes and socks and put them closer to the fire, trying to dry them out.

Bits looked around at our construction job. "I never thought we could do this much so fast." She smiled. "You know, this isn't bad."

"It wasn't us." Tiny fed a thick limb into the fire. The flames crackled and leaped with blue-and-yellow sparkles. "It was God helping us. This is exactly what we prayed for, isn't it?"

"No," Mike said, "the houseboat is exactly what we prayed for."

"Yeah, but we also wanted Him to make sure Lisa was safe. She is. So are we. Was it you that asked Him to hold off with the rain? Well, He did."

"Oh, for pity sake! You people were the ones that did it!" Lisa protested. "If you didn't have pocketknives and didn't know just what to do, we'd be getting wet and cold now."

"I'm not going to argue with you." Tiny looked from face to face. "Time we said thank you, huh?"

I'm sure that Lisa would have jumped up and marched off in another of her famous huffs, but it was really raining out there now. And besides, she couldn't march on her swollen ankle. You could tell she dearly wanted to, though.

Tiny led off with prayer as before, and we each thanked God from our various ways of looking at the situation. Lisa, naturally, said nothing. And, as I thought later, that was an improvement. At least she didn't bad-mouth us or make fun of prayer.

After Tiny ended the prayer time, Mike asked, "Lisa? Did you try yelling to get attention from the houseboat?"

"Not until I heard you guys."

Our yell having now been perfected, we used it. A couple minutes later we tried again. And again.

Nothing.

Nothing at all, except for the drumming rain.

22

I'm so hungry, the dog's in danger—if we had a dog." I watched the place where our fire's flames turned from orange tongues into black smoke.

Mike sat cross-legged with his chin propped in his hands. "I got a sneaking suspicion this is gonna be a real, real long night."

Bits moped. "Real, real, real long."

We lapsed into silence and stared at the fire.

Splack! Lynn slapped at still another mosquito.

Now you may know that Minnesota has a humongous reputation for killer mosquitoes. And you may have noticed that up until now I never mentioned them. That's because on the houseboat we used all sorts of methods to keep them away. So they were never a problem.

Lisa used DEET, a powerful chemical, which is good. But Mom didn't think that the safety of DEET, especially on kids, was very well shown. So she didn't want us to use it. Her choice was garlic. She heard that if you eat lots of garlic, mosquitoes will leave you alone. Of course, with breath like that, all the rest of the world will leave you alone, too. We learned almost instantly that Minnesota mosquitoes just love garlic. Mom switched to an Avon product, and it did pretty well.

Mike swore by his favorite grandmother's old standby, used fabric-softener sheets. You rub them on exposed skin, and bugs stay off. He wasn't much bothered, so apparently it worked.

Dad liked Off.

I used the garlic and the Avon lotion and the Off and borrowed some fabric-softener sheets. I remained a smorgasbord for mosquitoes in spite of it all.

Anyway, by tonight, the day's mosquito repellants had all worn off. We didn't have any with us to replace them. Mosquitoes took note of that and closed in like wolves to the kill. You could hear their sharp little teeth clicking. I know—they don't have any teeth.

To top it off, we were wearing T-shirts. Bare arms. And poor old Tiny didn't even have that much anymore. As I said, smorgasbord.

Lynn asked, "Lisa? How did you end up out here on a rock in the middle of the woods?"

"You don't want to know. Besides, it's a long story."

"Yes, I do want to know. And we have a long night to hear it in."

"Long night isn't the half of it," I added. "Somebody will have to stay up all night to feed the fire."

Lisa studied the flames a moment. "I really hate it when your parents send you out to spy on me, Les."

"I wasn't spying. I was finding you in case you were lost."

"Spying." She went on. "So when I came out this way from the houseboat, I decided to go extra far. Then I came to a big, wide, wet place. Marshy area. And I thought, *Les will think I wouldn't bother to go clear around this.* So I tried to go around it."

"Aha!" Bits roared. "We figured that!"

Lisa ignored her. "Then I got lost. I passed this rock. It sort of sits there all by itself. Then I passed another one. But it looked like this one. So I scraped a line in it. When I came to another rock fifteen minutes later, I looked for the mark. There it was. I was going in circles."

"Wow! Good show, Tiny!" Bits swatted his shoulder.

"So I decided to just sit and wait. I didn't know it was going to rain. If you guys hadn't found me, I'd be soaked now. And cold—it's really cold out there. It's better in here."

For a moment I saw a blue light out there in the woods. At first I thought it was someone with a flashlight coming toward us. Then thunder rumbled. Nope. Just a lightning storm.

Uh-oh. Lightning.

I asked, "What can we do about the lightning? What if it strikes near here? It could fry us."

"Yeah!" said Bits. "Every summer you read about cows or sheep that get under a tree to get away from the rain and stay dry, and then lightning strikes the tree, and they're all dead." When Bits got nervous or worried, she would start talking in very long sentences.

"Nothing we can do," Lynn said, "besides pray."

So we prayed right there, asking for protection and safety. Lynn led that one.

Lisa was watching us as we raised our heads. "I don't believe you guys! How nerdy can you get?"

"Fine!" Bits snapped. "If you don't want God to protect us, you do it! Go ahead. You do something to make us safe if lightning hits nearby." She paused. "Well?"

"But it's uncool to pray out loud in public! If you must—"

Bits exploded. "Who cares what's cool and uncool, Lisa? This is real life, not looking pretty. That's real rain out there and real thunder and lightning! And we're real lost, not playing camp out. And you worry about looking cool to a bunch of people who don't give a rip. You think you are such hot stuff! And you're so shallow!"

Lisa didn't say anything. Neither did anyone else.

Blue lightning flashed. It looked as if it was overhead, but lightning always does that. Thunder boomed a few seconds later.

Mike jumped, and Lisa reached out suddenly and wrapped an arm across his shoulders. She drew him in against her side.

And I realized where I had seen exactly that sort of thing happen before. It was during that thunderstorm when we were on the houseboat. When Dad and I stood on the back deck watching it, Mike came out. Dad held him exactly like that. Mike was frightened then, and that comforted him. He was surely frightened now. And Lisa saw that.

Maybe she wasn't as shallow as Bits claimed.

Lynn dug into her pocket. She fished out a pretty little stone with fairly sharp edges. "I found this along the shore. It's flint. See? Let's see if we can start a fire with it."

"We already have a fire," I reminded her, just in case she hadn't noticed.

"So I see. May I borrow your knife? I saw a how-to article in a magazine once."

And so, with Tiny providing tinder from the remote corners of our hotel suite—dry pine needles and lint from his pockets—and all of us giving her unwanted advice, Lynn tried to start a fire by striking the flint with a knife blade.

Don't believe everything you read in a how-to article.

23

Lisa watched Lynn trying in vain to make fire. "What are we going to do about breakfast?"

I answered, "Eat it."

"You know what I mean. Eat what? Berries?"

Tiny shook his head. "Berries aren't ripe yet. Maybe catch a turtle."

"Oh, yuck!"

"My Uncle Rafe says turtle's really good. He lives in Louisiana." Tiny smiled. "And he says that turtles even come in their own bowl. We'll think of something. Besides, they're out looking for us. We won't be here too long."

The fire-making attempt was a great way to keep our minds off the lightning. Finally the thunder grew more distant. The lightning passed. But the rain continued to pour.

Suddenly Lisa asked, "Did you guys really pray for me?"

"Somebody's got to." Bits shouldn't have said that, but I sure didn't blame her. I was extremely tired and starved and not in a very good mood myself.

Lisa didn't blow up for once. "What kinda Creek did you say?"

"Sugar," I said when I caught on. I sighed. "There we go talking about food again."

Lisa started to say something, but Tiny drowned her out with, "Let's yell again. We should do that every once in a while."

So we yelled and listened, and yelled and listened.

Not a thing.

Lisa asked suddenly, "You guys don't do any kissy face, do you?"

I bet you, if my stomach hadn't been so empty, I could have thrown up. Imagine, kissing girls!

Lisa didn't notice. "Or booze, either. I've been watching you really close. You guys have a real good time, and you don't have to drink or make out to do it."

Lynn studied her. "Where is this conversation going? We may not want to be there."

"I just told you. You have as much fun as my friends do, without that stuff. Maybe more." She hesitated. "I never saw anybody have a really good time without getting drunk before."

Mike believed her, obviously. "I wish you'd go down to Los Angeles and tell my Aunt Inez that. She drinks too much. My mama says, 'You don't need that,' but she does it anyway."

I believed her, too. And I just sat there openmouthed. In the first place, I couldn't imagine wanting to get drunk. What a waste. And I couldn't imagine what you'd do to have fun when you can't even think straight. I mean, you have to be able to think up fun things to do. That's half the fun of having fun, right?

Bits shook her head. "But, Lisa! You did not

have a good time on this trip! You didn't do much at all, except sunbathe. You complained the whole week long. The only thing you did a lot of was get out of working."

"That was the best Monopoly game I ever played. I love to be the banker, and no one ever lets me. I never went fishing before. Look what I caught! And, Les, your father was so patient. And your mom popped up with neat surprises, like those brownies. Most of all, I guess, you guys hate my guts, but you let me be one of you anyway."

"I wouldn't say 'hate your guts,' exactly." I tried to smooth it over.

It didn't work. Lisa laughed, and it was not a happy laugh. "When you gave me that left-over money, you made it plain enough. But see? Even though you hate me, you gave me your leftover money." Lisa stiffened a little. "Anyway, I'm going to try not to be such a . . . so grumpy."

"It doesn't matter, you know," Lynn said quietly.

I couldn't believe she said that! We all stared at her.

"You can be the most wonderful person in the world or the nastiest," Lynn explained. "Knowing Jesus is what gets you into heaven. Not behaving a particular way."

"I'll worry about heaven when I'm old."

"That's what lots of kids say who die before they're twenty."

Lisa glared at her. "You have an answer for everything, don't you!"

We all looked at Lynn, waiting to see what she'd come back with.

She sat watching Lisa, smiling, saying nothing at all.

Still glaring, Lisa called her a name that didn't fit Lynn a bit.

I sat and mulled all this over in my head awhile, and I thought I figured out a couple things. When the silence got too heavy to bear, I said, "I don't think you understand why we pray, Lisa. It's neat, but it's hard to explain. The Lord is so powerful it's terrifying, but He's a good friend. He's all kinds of contradictions like that. When we pray, we're not just asking Him for a favor. We're doing what He wants us to, the way He wants us to do it. He wants us to talk to Him and keep Him in mind. Keep Him number one. So that's what we try to do."

"Don't you tell me you do that all the time!"

"Not always. Sometimes I just don't think of Him when I should. But I try. All of us do. Anyway, Jesus' Spirit is in us, because we believe in Him. Within us. Inside us. However you want to say it. Praying helps us remember—keeps it on the front burner."

"That's so totally nerdy!" At least Lisa didn't call me a name. But then she said, "I never heard that before."

"Sure. That's because you only talk to 'cool' people, and praying isn't 'cool.' You just said so. Only there's some things more important than looking good in front of your friends. Being close friends with God is one of them."

Lisa snarled something. Then she stared at the fire, grumpy as a mole with a rash. "I don't know why I even bother talking to you people."

"Because you're stuck with us," Mike answered, "same as we're stuck with you. It isn't either one of us choosing each other. If we were at school, you wouldn't come near us. You wouldn't even think about us. And we'd stay on the other side of the cafeteria to stay away from you, because we think you're stuck-up."

Lisa snarled again. "I am not stuck-up! I'm particular about my friends, that's all!"

"Stuck-up. But here it's God throwing us all together on the same boat and in the same shelter." Mike grinned suddenly. "So you make do, eh?"

She snorted, maybe looking more amused now than angry.

I swatted yet another mosquito. "Look on the bright side, Lisa. This is going to give you all sorts of good stuff to write in your journal. You can complain for pages about getting prayed for. You can tell how you saved the day with that lighter. You did, too, you know. We couldn't have gotten a fire started without you. And it would be awfully dark and cold, even with the shelter, if we hadn't. And you can write down the plans for making a lean-to. And you can—"

"You've been reading my journal!"

"I don't even know where you keep it."

Bits smirked. "Why do you say that? You mean you already have instructions for making a lean-to in your journal?" Her voice hardened. "Your private life is your private life, Lisa. We're not the least bit interested in it. I'm just glad that it isn't mine."

"And what do you mean by that!"

"You're all screwed up, that's what I mean. My life is messed up because Mom left Dad. But it wasn't Dad's fault, and it wasn't mine. It was hers. I've figured that much out. So Dad and I do the best we can, and God takes care of what we can't manage by ourselves, because He loves us. But you! You screwed yourself up. You can't blame anybody but you."

"I am not screwed up!" Lisa yelled. "You are! And you're a geek, too!"

"So? I'm a happy geek," Bits said evenly. "Are you happy, Lisa?"

Oh, boy, was that ever bound to bring on a tirade! Lisa looked enraged. She opened her mouth.

And then the strangest thing happened. She just sat there with this odd look on her face. Her lower lip closed and opened again and quivered.

And then she murmured, "No," buried her face in her hands, and began to cry.

24

I get terribly embarrassed when somebody cries, unless that somebody is less than two years old. I looked around. I wasn't the only one, it appeared. Everybody just stared at the fire and tried to pretend that Lisa wasn't crying.

Everyone except Lynn. She got up and sat beside Lisa, with her back to the fire. When she wrapped an arm around Lisa's shoulders, Lisa didn't fight or pull away. So there they sat, one sobbing and the other simply holding.

Tiny said, "Let's try another shout."

The rest of us all gathered our lungs together and hollered. One, two, three, *yell!* One, two, three, *yell!*

When we paused between shouts to listen, all I could hear was the rain's quiet monologue.

Finally, Lisa wailed, "You want me to be a Jesus freak!"

"Freak, no. Safe in Jesus, yes." Lynn smiled. "We want the whole world to trust Jesus, Lisa. Not just you."

"But I don't want to be a nerd!"

Lynn asked, "Are you one now?"

"No!" Lisa seemed to be dragging her scattered parts back together. Sobs kept sneaking up on her, but she'd almost quit crying.

"Then you won't be one if you become a Christian. Even Paul in the Bible didn't really change his personality when he became a believer. The way he saw things changed is all."

Lisa sniffed and slurped some more.

Lynn sat erect. "Before I knew Jesus, I was good at math and lousy at sports. Now, I'm good at math and lousy at sports."

"I know. I've seen you at school."

"Fourth in the state in math scholarship tests, though, and it's my first year to take them. See? God uses what you are. You change into a better something, not into a nothing. A better person but not a different person." She twisted around to face the fire. "Tiny, what did God do to you?"

"I don't remember. I was a Christian since I was real young."

"Mike?"

He shrugged. "Now I like to go to church. Used to be, I'd try to get out of it. Worshiping God means something to me now. There's other stuff besides knowing I'm going to heaven."

I didn't want her to ask me that because I could not have answered. I seem to change every day. I learn stuff. I forget stuff. I do new things and do old things in new ways. But I didn't know what the changes in me were exactly. And I didn't really care. God was doing what He wanted with me, I was pretty certain. That was good enough for me.

Tiny spoke in that quiet way of his. "A lot of people call it being saved. You trust Jesus and belong to Him, and He keeps you from hell. That's what being saved means. But it doesn't mean much to the person who is not saved. They don't understand because they don't have the Spirit of God in them yet. The Bible says they can't see spiritual things well."

Lynn nodded. "I'd forgotten about that. When we talk about being saved and loved by God, it means something completely different to us than it does to Lisa. I wish we could help you, Lisa. Belonging to Jesus is the greatest thing in the world."

Lisa said quietly, "I watched Les's mom hold Catherine when she was sick. And I wished so hard that someone would hold me like that." She snorted. "I wish that now. I'm so scared and alone. But you people aren't."

"We're scared," I said.

"Not the same way. Not like I mean."

I didn't know exactly how she meant, so I just sat. We all sat.

Suddenly Lisa dug out her cigarettes. She tossed the pack into the fire.

I was about to cheer, but Mike yelped, "Listen!" He sat bolt upright and stared out into the wet blackness.

Now I could hear it, too. "That's not a person. It's gotta be an animal!"

"You're right!"

Quick as a flash, Tiny popped his pocket-knife open. We all did. Lynn didn't have a knife, so she snatched up a strong branch from the firewood pile.

An animal was shuffling through the forest duff. You could tell it was getting closer.

Lisa was so scared she shook. And the look on her face was pure terror.

Lynn pressed against one side of her. "Sit as close to the fire as you can. Fire scares animals. It won't come near. We'll protect you."

I sat on Lisa's other side. Tiny and Mike moved up by us. Bits manned the fort behind, lest some animal rip our shelter apart to get at us.

Bits said, "Look on the bright side, Lisa. It has five of us to eat before it gets to you."

This did not strike me as being all that reassuring.

"And even if we die, we're safe." Tiny shifted his weight a little.

Lisa moaned, absolutely terror struck.

I never felt more like running, either! Because now, out there in the blackness, two eyes glowed!

The thing came crashing toward us. The animal was black, because you couldn't see detail even though it was close.

A bear? Maybe a . . .

Gerty!

The old dog came bounding into the shelter and slobbered all over Lisa. And Lisa was sobbing again, and laughing, as she hugged her dog.

Only this time her sobbing didn't embarrass me at all. Because with Gerty here, Mom or Dad would surely be right behind!

It was Dad. He came sauntering in, in no hurry at all, talking on his cell phone. His yellow slicker glistened in the firelight.

"Yeah," he told the phone. "They're all here. They built a fire and made themselves a shelter. It looks like they're warmer and drier than I am right now."

He listened to his phone a minute. "That's right. So you can tell the rangers they're found and everything's fine." He listened again. "About fifteen minutes, twenty at most."

He pocketed his phone, and we all hugged him.

Tears were running down Lynn's face. "We're safe. We're found."

Lisa slurped her nose. "Yes. I think I am."

Other Sugar Creek Gang books:

The New Sugar Creek Gang #1

When he and his family move to the neighborhood surrounding Sugar Creek, 11-year old Les decides to explore where all those exciting old adventures happened. But by that night, Les is caught up in a mystery of his own.

ISBN#0-8024-8661-4

The New Sugar Creek Gang #2

After Les and Bits's church is set on fire, one of the Sugar Creek Gang starts acting awfully suspicious. Worst off all, a one-of-a-kind bike places the Sugar Creeker at the scene of the crime! Now it's up to the new Sugar Creek Gang to find a way to stand by their friend—and to solve the mystery before its too late!

ISBN#0-8024-8662-2

The New Sugar Creek Gang #3

When turkeys, deer and other creatures around Sugar Creek begin to turn up wounded, rumor has it wolves are to blame. Worried about the injured animals and their human neighbors, the New Sugar Creek Gang vows to get to the bottom of the mystery.

ISBN# 0-8024-8663-0

The New Sugar Creek Gang #4

After Lynn wins a dinosaur-drawing contest, the New Sugar Creek Gang gets to join a real, honest-to-goodness dinosaur dig in Arizona! When important items start disappearing from the site, it looks like the kids may be sent home unless the gang can solve the mystery and save the day!

ISBN# 0-8024-8664-9